OPEN CITY

New York City, Summer 2009
Number Twenty-Seven

 **OPEN CITY**

Actual Air
Poems by David Berman

"David Berman's poems are beautiful, strange, intelligent, and funny. They are narratives that freeze life in impossible contortions. They take the familiar and make it new, so new the reader is stunned and will not soon forget. I found much to savor on every page of *Actual Air*. It's a book for everyone."
 —James Tate

"This is the voice I have been waiting so long to hear . . . Any reader who tunes in to his snappy, offbeat meditations is in for a steady infusion of surprises and delights."
 —Billy Collins

My Misspent Youth
Essays by Meghan Daum

"An empathic reporter and a provocative autobiographer . . . I finished it in a single afternoon, mesmerized and sputtering."
 —*The Nation*

"Meghan Daum articulates the only secret left in the culture: discreet but powerful fantasies of romance, elegance, and ease that survive in our uncomfortable world of striving. These essays are very smart and very witty and just heartbreaking enough to be deeply pleasurable."
 —Marcelle Clements

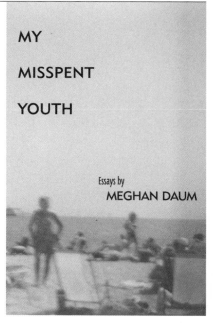

BOOKS

Venus Drive
Stories by Sam Lipsyte

"Sam Lipsyte is a wickedly gifted writer. *Venus Drive* is filled with grimly satisfying fractured insights and hardcore humor. But it also displays some inspired sympathy for the daze and confusion of its characters. Above all it's wonderfully written and compulsively readable with brilliant and funny dialogue, a collection that represents the emergence of a very strong talent."
   —Robert Stone

"Sam Lipsyte can get blood out of a stone—rich, red human blood from the stony sterility of contemporary life. His writing is gripping—at least I gripped this book so hard my knuckles turned white."
   —Edmund White

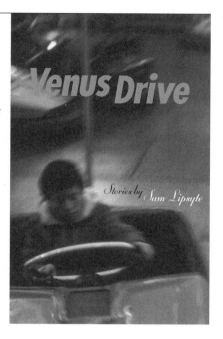

Karoo
A Novel by Steve Tesich

"Fascinating—a real satiric invention full of wise outrage."
   —Arthur Miller

"A powerful and deeply disturbing portrait of a flawed, self-destructive, and compulsively fascinating figure."
   —*Kirkus Reviews* (starred)

"Saul Karoo is a new kind of wild man, the sane maniac. Larger than life and all too human, his out-of-control odyssey through sex, death, and show business is extreme, and so is the pleasure of reading it. Steve Tesich created a fabulously Gargantuan comic character."
   —Michael Herr

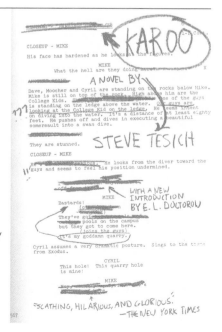

Some Hope
A Trilogy by Edward St. Aubyn

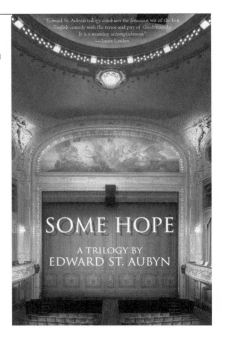

"Tantalizing . . . A memorable tour de force."
 —*The New York Times Book Review*

"Hilarious and harrowing by turns, sophisticated, reflective, and brooding."
 —*The New York Review of Books*

"Feverishly good writing . . . Full of Algonquin wit on the surface while roiling underneath. *Some Hope* is a hell of a brew, as crisp and dry as a good English cider and as worth savoring as any of Waugh's most savage volleys."
 —*The Ruminator Review*

Mother's Milk
A Novel by Edward St. Aubyn

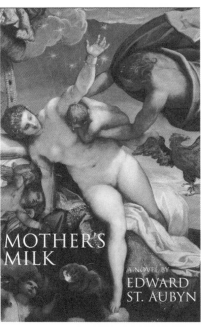

"St. Aubyn's caustic, splendid novel probes the slow violence of blood ties—a superbly realized agenda hinted at in the novel's arresting first sentence: 'Why had they pretended to kill him when he was born?'"
 —*The Village Voice*

"Postpartum depression, assisted suicide, adultery, alcoholism—it's all here in St. Aubyn's keenly observed, perversely funny novel about an illustrious cosmopolitan family and the mercurial matriarch who rules them all."
 —*People*

BOOKS

Goodbye, Goodness
A Novel by Sam Brumbaugh

"*Goodbye, Goodness* is the rock n' roll *Great Gatsby.*"
  —*New City Chicago*

"Sam Brumbaugh's debut novel couldn't be more timely. *Goodbye, Goodness* boasts just enough sea air and action to make an appealing summer read without coming anywhere near fluffsville."
  —*Time Out New York*

"Beautifully captures the wrung-out feel of a depleted American century."
  —*Baltimore City Paper*

"Brumbaugh takes us to the burnt-out edges of personal history. He is able to watch and observe and feel at the same time—a fact finder stuck in a tragicomedy, with slow acoustic guitar as a sidekick."
—Stephen Malkmus

Goodbye,
Goodness
a novel by
Sam Brumbaugh

The First Hurt
Stories by Rachel Sherman

"Sherman's writing is sharp, hard, and honest; there's a fearlessness in her work, an I'm-not-afraid-to-say-this quality. Because she knows that most of us have thought the same but didn't have the guts to say it."
  —*Boston Phoenix*

"Rachel Sherman writes stories like splinters: they get under your skin and stay with you long after you've closed the book. These haunting stories are both wonderfully, deeply weird and unsettlingly familiar."
  —*Judy Budnitz*

The First Hurt
Stories by Rachel Sherman

 **OPEN CITY**

Long Live a Hunger to Feed Each Other
Poems by Jerome Badanes

"Reading Jerome Badanes's poems is
not so much reading a voice from the
heartfelt past as reading a poet whose
work is very much alive and yet reflects
a lost—and meaningful—age. He is
one of our good souls; he is one of our
poets. I treasure his work."
—Gerald Stern

"The best best book publishing story of
the year."
—*Poetry*

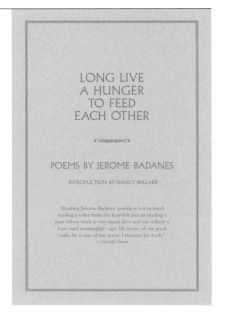

Farewell Navigator
Stories by Leni Zumas

"Zumas gives socially awkward, mysteri-
ously gifted and self-destructive outcasts
spellbinding, unflinching voice. . . . It's
a powerful, irresistible collection."
—*Publishers Weekly*

"Leni Zumas's writing is fearless and
swift, sassy and sensational."
—Joy Williams

"I have never read stories like these
before and I can't get them out of my
head. Her language is real sorcery—it
dismantles the world you think you
know and takes you to strange, fecund
territories of the imagination. "
—Karen Russell

BOOKS

Love Without
Stories by Jerry Stahl

"[Stahl]...knows how to shock us into laughter, and his best work mines the grotesque for pathos, a tradition that includes Flannery O'Connor, Barry Hannah, and Denis Johnson . . .The key isn't whom he writes about, but at what depth . . . Stahl plunges us into depraved worlds with a keen intensity of purpose, and his addled protagonists run up hard against the truth of their desires."
—Los Angeles Times

"Tender and gut-busting."
—L.A. Weekly

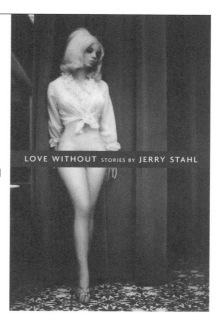

Why the Devil Chose New England for His Work
Stories by Jason Brown

"*Why the Devil Chose New England for His Work* links gem-cut stories of troubled youths, alcoholics, illicit romances, the burden of inheritance, and the bane of class, all set in the dense upper reaches of Maine, and delivers them with hope, heart, and quiet humor."
—Lisa Shea, *Elle*

OPEN CITY BOOKS

Summer 2009
Flight Patterns
Edited by Dorothy Spears

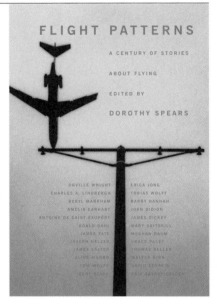

This anthology of stories about air travel features writing by: Orville Wright, Charles A. Lindbergh, James Salter, Mary Gaitskill, Tobias Wolff, Grace Paley, Walter Kirn, Alice Munro, Jerry Stahl, Antione de Saint Exupèry, Thomas Beller, Tom Wolfe, Joseph Heller, James Dickey, Erica Jong, Saïd Sayrafiezadeh, Roald Dahl, Meghan Daum, Barry Hannah, Beryl Markham, Mary Lee Settle, Amelia Earhart, Sheila M. Schwartz, Manuel Gonzales, Jonathan Tel, Rachel Cantor, Bernard Chabbert, John Bowe, Gary Horn, Brad Kessler, and Linda Yablonsky.

Fall 2009
Living Room
A Novel by Rachel Sherman

"A compelling and unsentimental novel about the loneliness that exists just below the surface of a family. Sherman skillfully and movingly renders the inner lives of three generations of women as they try—or don't try—to reconcile the distance between their desires and their actual lives."
  —Dana Spiotta

"*Living Room* is edgy, moving, smart, funny and altogether human. Rachel Sherman is the real deal."
  —Dani Shapiro

OPEN CITY

A personal and entertaining reflection on Susan Sontag— from renowned essayist Phillip Lopate

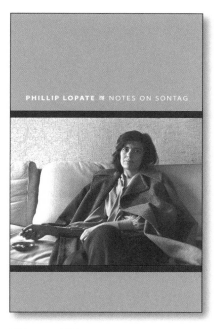

Writers on Writers
Cloth $19.95 978-0-691-13570-0

Notes on Sontag
Phillip Lopate

Notes on Sontag is a frank, witty, and entertaining reflection on the work, influence, and personality of one of the "foremost interpreters of . . . our recent contemporary moment." Adopting Sontag's favorite form, a set of brief essays or notes that circle around a topic from different perspectives, renowned essayist Phillip Lopate considers the achievements and limitations of his tantalizing, daunting subject through what is fundamentally a conversation between two writers.

"Lopate and Sontag are an inspired pairing. Lopate has just the right distance on Sontag—neither sycophant nor peer—to write trenchantly and sympathetically about her achievements, but he's also unsparing about her occasional idiocies. Some of the best things in the book are the personal vignettes about close encounters with Sontag, where Lopate stands in for the reader and fan, often getting burned in the process."

—Christopher Benfey, Mount Holyoke College

OPEN CITY

Open City is published by Open City, Inc., a nonprofit corporation. Donations are tax-deductible to the extent allowed by the law. A one-year subscription (3 issues) is $30; a two-year subscription (6 issues) is $55. Make checks payable to: Open City, Inc., 270 Lafayette Street, Suite 1412, New York, NY 10012. For credit-card orders, see our Web site: www.opencity.org. E-mail: editors@opencity.org.

Open City is a member of the Council of Literary Magazines and Presses and is indexed by Humanities International Complete.

Open City gratefully acknowledges the generous support of the family of Robert Bingham. We also thank the New York State Council on the Arts, a state agency. See the page following the masthead for additional donor acknowledgments.

NYSCA

Front and back covers by Karen Green. Front: *Mrs. John White Alexander* (from the "Imagine Them Naked" series), sumi ink on rice paper, player piano music, vintage paper, coffee filter, 2007. Back: *Oak*, sumi ink, wax, oil paint on vintage papers, 2007.

Front page photograph by Jocko Weyland, *High Line Trains*, 2009.

Elliott Puckette's images (pp. 29–34) appear courtesy of Paul Kasmin Gallery.

ISBN-13: 978-1-890447-52-6
ISBN-10: 1-890447-52-8
ISSN: 1089-5523

OPEN CITY

EDITORS
Thomas Beller
Joanna Yas

ART DIRECTOR
Nick Stone

EDITOR-AT-LARGE
Adrian Dannatt

CONTRIBUTING EDITORS
Jonathan Ames
Elizabeth Beller
David Berman
Aimée Bianca
Will Blythe
Jason Brown
Sam Brumbaugh
Patrick Gallagher
Amanda Gersh
Laura Hoffmann
Jan de Jong
Kip Kotzen
Anthony Lacavaro
Vanessa Lilly
Sam Lipsyte
Jim Merlis
Honor Moore
Parker Posey
Beatrice von Rezzori
Elizabeth Schmidt
Lee Smith
Dorothy Spears
Maxine Swann
Alexandra Tager
Tony Torn
Jocko Weyland
Edmund White

DEVELOPMENT DIRECTOR
Kimberly King Parsons

INTERNS
Joanna Bock
Sarah Clark
Emily Hunt
Rowland Miller

READERS
Mike Gardner
Evan Hansen
Michael Hornburg
Sarah LaPolla
Lina Makdisi
Ana Saldamando

FOUNDING EDITORS
Thomas Beller
Daniel Pinchbeck

FOUNDING PUBLISHER
Robert Bingham

OPEN CITY WOULD LIKE TO THANK THE FOLLOWING FOR THEIR GENEROUS CONTRIBUTIONS

Patrons ($1,000 or more)
Clara Bingham
Joan Bingham
Belle & Henry Davis
Wendy Flanagan
Laura Fontana & John J. Moore
Laura Hoffmann
Alex Kuczynski
Vanessa & John Lilly
Eleanor & Rowland Miller
Scott Smith
Dorothy Spears
Mary & Jeffrey Zients

Donors ($500 or more)
Robert Scott Asen
Hava Beller
David Selig (Rice Restaurant)
Amine Wefali (Zaitzeff Restaurant)

Contributors ($150 or more)

Henry Alcalay
Molly Bingham
Duncan Birmingham
Paula Bomer
Nina Collins
Joe Conason & Elizabeth Wagley
Paula Cooper
Holly Dando
Edward Garmey
David Goodwillie
Pierre Hauser
Carol Irving
Kathy Kemp

Jason Kliot & Joana Vicente
Caitlin Macy & Jeremy Barnum
William Morton
Rulonna Neilson
Tim Nye
Rick Rofihe
Robert Soros &
    Melissa Schiff Soros
Jennifer Sturman
Judson Traphagan
Elizabeth Wagley & Joe Conason
Shelley Wanger
Chris Young

Friends

Alex Abramovich
Jonathan Ames
Lucy Anderson
Tony Antoniadis
Harold Augenbraum
Noah Baumbach
Madeleine Beckman
Madison Smartt Bell
Elizabeth Beller
Betsy Berne
Aimée Bianca
Andrew Blauner
Ghurron Briscoe
Sam Brumbaugh
Toby Bryce
Jocelyn Casey-Whitman
Simon Constable
Thomas Cregan
Adrian Dannatt
John Donahue
Christopher Edgar
Erin Edmison
Deborah Eisenberg
Lisa Evanchuck
Mary Evans
Jofie Ferrari-Adler
Mike Gardner
Deborah Garrison
Alice Gordon
Melissa Gould
Melissa Grace
Rebecca Green
Will Heinrich
Jessamyn Hope
Gerald Howard
Amy Hundley
Anthony Lacavaro
Deborah Landau

Matt Lee
Guy Lesser
Sam Lipsyte
Stephen Mark
Pearson Marx
Vestal McIntyre
Paul Morris
Carolyn Murnick
Christopher Nicholson
Ethan Nosowsky
Nancy Novogrod
Sylvia Paret
Vince Passaro
Francine Prose
Beatrice von Rezzori
Anne Rivers
Saïd Sayrafiezadeh
Elizabeth Schmidt
Richard Serra
Wallace Shawn
Rachel Sherman
Claudia Silver
Debra Singer
Betsy Smith
Lee Smith
Valerie Steiker
Anna Stein
Ben Stiller
Nick Stone
Robert Stone
Stefanie Syman
Paul Tullis
Ben Turner
Dean Wareham & Britta Phillips
Cecilia & John Weyland
Malerie Willens
Leni Zumas
Todd Zuniga

NEW FROM VESTAL McINTYRE

"Every character in *Lake Overturn* is so real, complex, and interesting, the scope of the novel at once so wide and so deep, the themes and ideas so thoroughly embodied by the story, I felt as if I were reading a modern-day *Middlemarch*."

–Kate Christensen, PEN/Faulkner Award-winning author of *The Great Man*

"For nearly thirty years now we've been told that we are divided by religion and by region–Christian fundamentalists against secular progressives, the rural middle against the urban coast–and across the divide we've stared at one another, aided in our vision by little more than clichés. What a great relief, then, to read Vestal McIntyre's splendid first novel, which renders such simplifications obsolete one character at a time, giving us instead, in all their broken, human form, the single mothers living in the respectable half of the trailer park and their brainy, lovelorn kids and perhaps McIntyre's finest creation– the drug-addled sister of the school bus driver who longs to bear a child (she will break your heart). ***Lake Overturn* is loving and searing and sad and, above all, a pleasure to read."**

–Adam Haslett, author of *You Are Not a Stranger Here*

18 17

HARPER

An Imprint of HarperCollins*Publishers*
www.harpercollins.com

ANNA

CLOTHES FOR WOMEN

150 East 3rd Street at Avenue A
New York City
212.358.0195
www.annanyc.com

ACADEMY AWARD® NOMINEE

"Forceful and important...gripping."
–The New York Times

The
RESTLESSCONSCIENCE
RESISTANCE TO HITLER IN NAZI GERMANY
A Film by Hava Kohav Beller

"Graceful...Devastating...
It's a provocative examination of ethics put to the gravest test imaginable."
– The Wall Street Journal

AVAILABLE NOW
ON DVD, ITUNES, AND NETFLIX

" . . .Very moving documentary . . . fascinating . . . intense and powerful."
—**Georgia Brown,** *The Village Voice*

"Hava Kohav Beller's remarkable, Oscar-nominated documentary about anti-Nazi resistance in Germany between 1933 and 1945 is a heartbreaking historical work . . . Fictional accounts pale by comparison."
—**Hal Hinson,** *The Washington Post*

" . . . A compelling work of historical and human significance."
—**John Kenneth Galbraith**

"The film has passion and depth that is rare in documentaries today."
—**Richard Hutton, WNET/Thirteen**

"Tough, impassioned document . . . vivid, heartbreaking . . . powerful and important."
—**Edward Guthmann,** *San Francisco Chronicle*

"Devastating . . . deeply affecting . . . unique."
—**David Armstrong,** *San Francisco Examiner*

"Hava Kohav Beller's gripping documentary . . . is a powerful piece of work."
—**Harry Haun,** *The Daily News*

"A fresh moral perspective on Nazism's trajectory . . . The film's value can scarcely be overstated . . . Searing and unforgettable power."
—**Godfrey Cheshire,** *New York Press*

www.therestlessconscience.com

anderbo.com "Best New Online Journal"
—storySouth Million Writers Award

anderbo.com

fiction   poetry   "fact"   photography

RROFIHE TROPHY!

FOR AN UNPUBLISHED SHORT STORY
(UP TO 5,000 WORDS)

WINNER RECEIVES:
$500 CASH
TROPHY
PUBLICATION IN OPEN CITY

JUDGED BY RICK ROFIHE

2009 RRofihe Trophy Guidelines

- Stories should be typed, double-spaced, on 8 1/2 x 11 paper with the author's name and contact information on the first page and name and story title on the upper right corner of remaining pages
- Submissions must be postmarked by October 15, 2009
- Limit one submission per author
- Author must not have been previously published in *Open City*
- Mail submissions to RRofihe, 270 Lafayette Street, Suite 1412, New York, NY 10012
- Enclose self-addressed stamped business envelope to receive names of winner and honorable mentions
- All manuscripts are non-returnable and will be recycled
- Reading fee is $10. Check or money order payable to RRofihe
- Judged by Rick Rofihe; 2009 Contest Assistant: Carolyn Wilsey

www.opencity.org/rrofihe

"Beautifully crafted,
at once elegant and astonishing.
Highly recommended."
—LIBRARY JOURNAL (STARRED REVIEW)

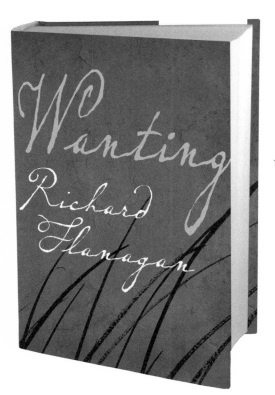

"*Wanting* shakes us rudely
from our stupors,
wakes us up to history.
There can be no author
more passionate or
unfettered than Flanagan."
—SYDNEY MORNING HERALD

"[Flanagan's] prose is
strong and precise,
and the depiction of desire's
effects is sublime."
—PUBLISHERS WEEKLY

In his new novel, the author of the acclaimed *Gould's Book of Fish* tells of a young Aboriginal girl adopted by the most celebrated explorer of the age, Sir John Franklin, and his wife, Lady Jane, to demonstrate that the primitive can be civilized. Years later, Sir John disappears on a search for the Northwest Passage, and Lady Jane turns to the great novelist Charles Dickens—a man of passion locked in an icebound marriage—to defend her husband against shocking accusations of savagery.

FINALIST FOR
THE MILES FRANKLIN LITERARY AWARD

 ATLANTIC MONTHLY PRESS
an imprint of Grove/Atlantic, Inc.
Distributed by Publishers Group West
www.groveatlantic.com

LOST AND FOUND

STORIES FROM NEW YORK, VOL. II

EDITED BY
THOMAS BELLER

Essays from Mr. Beller's Neighborhood by:

Charles D'Ambrosio, Rachel Cline, Meghan Daum,
Hal Sirowitz, Matthew Roberts, Debbie Nathan, Saïd
Sayrafiezadeh, Rachel Sherman, Bryan Charles,
Phillip Lopate, Jonathan Ames, Alicia Erian,
Madison Smartt Bell, Betsy Berne, Thomas Beller,
Sam Lipsyte, and more.

Spring 2009
Mr. Beller's Neighborhood Books
Distributed by W.W. Norton

www.mrbellersneighborhood.com

CONTRIBUTORS' NOTES

PATRICIA BOSWORTH is the author of biographies of Montgomery Clift, Diane Arbus, Marlon Brando, and Jane Fonda (forthcoming). She is also the author of a memoir about her family entitled *Any Little Thing Your Heart Desires*. After working as an actress in the fifties, Bosworth switched to journalism, and was an editor at *Woman's Day*, *McCall's*, and *Harper's Bazaar*. She is currently a contributing editor at *Vanity Fair* and lives in New York City.

BRYAN CHARLES is the author of the novel *Grab On to Me Tightly as if I Knew the Way*. He recently completed a memoir, from which the piece in this issue is excerpted. He's at work on a book about the Pavement album *Wowee Zowee* for the 33 1/3 series.

BILLY COLLINS is the author of numerous poetry collections, including *The Art of Drowning*, and, most recently, *Ballistics*. Born in New York City in 1941, Collins has received multiple awards and honors—among these a two-term appointment as the U.S. Poet Laureate (2001–2003). He lives in Somers, New York.

LOUISE DESPONT is a French-American artist living in Brooklyn. Her work is represented by Nicelle Beauchene Gallery in New York.

CJ EVANS's chapbook, *The Category of Outcast,* was selected by Terrance Hayes to receive the 2008 Poetry Society of America's New York Chapbook Fellowship, and his poems have appeared, or are forthcoming, in journals such as *AGNI Online, Denver Quarterly, Gulf Coast, Pleiades, LIT,* and *Virginia Quarterly Review*. He's the co-editor of *Satellite Convulsions: Poems from Tin House*, and the associate poetry editor at *Tin House* magazine.

KAREN GREEN lives and works out of her studio/gallery, Beautiful Crap, in Claremont, California. Her book, *Here/Gone*, an alphabet flip book for grownups, was published by Spineless Books in October 2008.

A. M. HOMES is the author of the novels *This Book Will Save Your Life, Music for Torching, The End of Alice, In a Country of Mothers,* and *Jack*; the short story collections *The Safety of Objects* and *Things You Should Know*; and a memoir, *The Mistress's Daughter.* Among her many awards are Guggenheim and NEA fellowships.

JASON LABBE's poems appear in recent or forthcoming issues of *Poetry, American Letters & Commentary, Court Green, The Hat, Barrow Street, Vanitas*, and other journals. He divides his time between Bethany, Connecticut, and Brooklyn, New York.

ZACHARY LAZAR is the author of two novels, most recently *Sway,* about the rise and fall of the 1960s counterculture. A nonfiction novel, *Evening's Empire: The Story of My Father's Murder*, will be published by Little, Brown in November of 2009. Lazar is a 2009–10 Hodder Fellow at Princeton University and has also won a Guggenheim Fellowship.

DAVID JAICKS lives and works in the hills of western Massachusetts with a golden retriever named Willy.

GREG LIPPMAN divides his time between Paris and New York City, where he works part time as a pro bono attorney at The Innocence Project, the criminal DNA exonerations concern. His play, *Paradox Lust,* was produced off-Broadway in 2001; his latest play, *Fiber Head*, was just given a first reading at Naked Angels. The pieces here are from a collection entitled *Stories for People with a Modern Attention Span*.

CHRISTOPHER de LOTBINIÈRE, a British painter and printmaker, has been living in New York since 1995. He is currently working on a series of paintings and prints inspired by the classical ideals of Italian Renaissance and their effect on English architecture of the eighteenth century.

EVA MARER was born in 1969 in Bloomington, Indiana. Daughter of a German mother and a Hungarian father, she grew up speaking three languages. After graduating from college, she moved to Paris where she added a fourth language to her repertoire and taught SAT courses to French nationals. She subsequently returned to the United States and enrolled in Columbia University's Journalism school. After graduating, she worked as a freelance journalist, publishing in *Vogue*, *SELF*, *Health*, *Woman's Day,* and *Marie Claire*, among many other magazines. She passed away in January of this year. This is her first fiction publication.

VESTAL McINTYRE was born and raised in Nampa, Idaho, and has lived in Boston and New York City. His story collection, *You Are Not the One*, won a Lambda Literary Award and earned him fellowships in fiction from the National Endowment for the Arts and the New York Foundation for the Arts. His stories have appeared in many publications, including *Open City* 11 and 22. He now lives in London and has recently published a novel entitled *Lake Overturn*.

ELLIOTT PUCKETTE was born in Lexington, Kentucky. She lives and works in New York City, where she is represented by Paul Kasmin Gallery.

TOMAŽ ŠALAMUN's books of poetry have been translated into most of the European languages. He lives in Ljubljana and occasionally teaches in the United States. His recent books translated into English are *Woods and Chalices*, *Poker*, and *There's the Hand and There's the Arid Chair*. *Blue Tower* is forthcoming in 2010.

AUDREY SALMON was born in Lyon in 1977. Upon graduation from the Ecole des Arts Appliqués she worked for the French advertising firm SJM before moving to China and settling in Beijing. Her photographs were included in the "Invitation au Voyage" exhibition that traveled to Hong Kong, Singapore, and Taipei. FakeSpace in Beijing presented a solo show of the "Mutant Architecture" series in 2008.

STEPHEN CAMPBELL SUTHERLAND was born in Florida and schooled in the United States and England before reading philosophy and theology at Oxford. He has subsequently lived in Berlin, Manhattan, West Africa, and Chiang Mai, where he taught at the university. He presently divides his time between rural Suffolk and London.

EDMUND WHITE is a novelist, memoirist, and biographer. He is the author of many books including *A Boy's Own Story*, *The Married Man*, *The Flâneur*, and biographies of Marcel Proust and Jean Genet (winner of the National Book Critics Circle Award). His memoir *City Boy: My Life in New York During the 1960s and 70s*, from which the piece in this issue is excerpted, is forthcoming in the fall. He is also a professor of creative writing at Princeton.

DARA WIER is the author of ten poetry collections; her *Selected Poems* is forthcoming from Wave Books this fall. Born in Louisiana, she is currently the director of the MFA writing program at the University of Massachusetts.

HEADY TIMES ALONG THE GRAND CONCOURSE

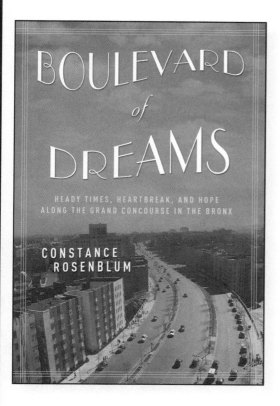

❝ For anyone who has ever loved a great street or neighborhood as change after change swept over it and dreams and challenges converged. So in fact this is a book for anyone who has ever lived anywhere. It's a rich, sometimes wild ride through a century of history, beautifully written by a gifted observer. **❞**

—**TONY HISS,** author of *The Experience of Place*

❝ Rosenblum writes with deep feeling and an acute eye but she is unflinching and the result is a book that does far more than invite nostalgia. *Boulevard of Dreams* helped me revise and enrich memories of my own childhood. **❞**

—**LAURA SHAINE CUNNINGHAM,** author of *Sleeping Arrangements*

$27.95 CLOTH / 256 PAGES / 44 ILLUSTRATIONS

Stretching over four miles through the center of the West Bronx, the Grand Boulevard and Concourse, known simply as the Grand Concourse, has gracefully served as silent witness to the changing face of the Bronx, and New York City, for a century.

Now, to coincide with the Concourse's centennial, Constance Rosenblum (a *New York Times* editor) brings to life the street in all its raucous glory. This is a must read for anyone interested in the rich history of the twentieth-century American city.

NICK STONE DESIGN

50 Pine Street #5S New York, NY 10005

stone@nickstonedesign.com

www.nickstonedesign.com

T: 212.995.1863

F: 212.353.0592

M: 718.791.3960

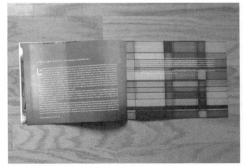

LINCOLN PLAZA CINEMAS

Six Screens

63RD STREET & BROADWAY
OPPOSITE LINCOLN CENTER
212-757-2280

OPEN

"The Crazy Person" by Mary Gaitskill, "La Vie en Rose" by Hubert Selby Jr., "Cathedral Parkway" by Vince Passaro. Art by Jeff Koons and Devon Dikeou. Cover by Ken Schles, whose *Invisible City* sells for thousands on Ebay. Stan Friedman's poems about baldness and astronomy, Robert Polito on Lester Bangs, Jon Tower's real life letters to astronauts. (Vastly underpriced at $400. Only two copies left.)

A first glimpse of Martha McPhee; a late burst from Terry Southern. Jaime Manrique's "Twilight at the Equator." Art by Paul Ramirez-Jonas, Kate Milford, Richard Serra. Kip Kotzen's "Skate Dogs," Richard Foreman's "Poetry City" with playful illustrations by Daniel Pinchbeck, David Shields' "Sports" and his own brutal youth. (Ken Schles found the negative of our cover girl on Thirteenth Street and Avenue B. We're still looking for the girl. $25)

Irvine Welsh's "Eurotrash" (his American debut), Richard Yates (from his last, unfinished novel), Patrick McCabe (years before *The Butcher Boy*). Art by Francesca Woodman (with an essay by Betsy Berne), Jacqueline Humphries, Allen Ginsberg, Alix Lambert. A short shot of Lipsyte—"Shed"—not available anywhere else. Plus Alfred Chester's letters to Paul Bowles. Chip Kidd riffs on the Fab Four. (Very few copies left! $25)

Stories by the always cheerful Cyril Connolly ("Happy Deathbeds"), Thomas McGuane, Jim Thompson, Samantha Gillison, Michael Brownstein, and Emily Carter, whose "Glory Goes and Gets Some" was reprinted in *Best American Short Stories.* Art by Julianne Swartz and Peter Nadin. Poems by David Berman and Nick Tosches. Plus Denis Johnson in Somalia. (A monster issue, sales undercut by slightly rash choice of cover art by editors. Get it while you can! $15)

Change or Die
Stories by David Foster Wallace, Siobhan Reagan, Irvine Welsh. Jerome Badanes' brilliant novella, "Change or Die" (film rights still available). Poems by David Berman and Vito Acconci. Plus Helen Thorpe on the murder of Ireland's most famous female journalist, and Delmore Schwartz on T. S. Eliot's squint. (Still sold-out! Wait for e-books to catch on or band together and demand a reprint.)

CITY back issues

The Only Woman He's Ever Left
Stories by James Purdy, Jocko Weyland, Strawberry Saroyan. Michael Cunningham's "The Slap of Love." Poems by Rick Moody, Deborah Garrison, Monica Lewinsky, Charlie Smith. Art by Matthew Ritchie, Ellen Harvey, Cindy Stefans. Rem Koolhaas project. With a beautiful cover by Adam Fuss. (Only $10 for this blockbuster.)

ISSUE #6

The Rubbed Away Girl
Stories by Mary Gaitskill, Bliss Broyard, and Sam Lipsyte. Art by Jimmy Raskin, Laura Larson, and Jeff Burton. Poems by David Berman, Elizabeth Macklin, Stephen Malkmus, and Will Oldham. (We found some copies in the back of the closet so were able to lower the price! $25 (it *was* $50))

ISSUE #7

Beautiful to Strangers
Stories by Caitlin O'Connor Creevy, Joyce Johnson, and Amine Wefali, back when her byline was Zaitzeff (now the name of her organic sandwich store at Nassau & John Streets—go there for lunch!). Poems by Harvey Shapiro, Jeffrey Skinner, and Daniil Kharms. Art by David Robbins, Liam Gillick, and Elliott Puckette. Piotr Uklanski's cover is a panoramic view of Queens, shot from the top of the World Trade Center in 1998. ($10)

ISSUE #8

Bewitched
Stories by Jonathan Ames, Said Shirazi, and Sam Lipsyte. Essays by Geoff Dyer and Alexander Chancellor, who hates rabbit. Poems by Chan Marshall, Lucy Anderson, and Edvard Munch on intimate and sensitive subjects. Art by Karen Kilimnick, Giuseppe Penone, Mark Leckey, Maurizio Cattelan, and M.I.M.E. (Our bestselling issue. ($10))

ISSUE #9

Editors' Issue
Previously demure editors publish themselves. Enormous changes at the last minute. Stories by Robert Bingham, Thomas Beller, Daniel Pinchbeck, Joanna Yas, Adrian Dannatt, Kip Kotzen, Geoffrey O' Brien, Lee Smith, Amanda Gersh, and Jocko Weyland. Poems by Tony Torn. Art by Nick Stone, Meghan Gerety, and Alix Lambert. (Years later, Ken Schles's cover photo appears on a Richard Price novel.) ($10)

ISSUE #10

OPEN

Octo Ate Them All
Vestal McIntyre emerges from the slush pile like aphrodite
with a brilliant story that corresponds to the tattoo that
covers his entire back. Siobhan Reagan thinks about
strangulation. Fiction by Melissa Pritchard and Bill Broun.
Anthropologist Michael Taussig's Cocaine Museum. Gregor
von Rezzori's meditation on solitude, sex, and raw meat.
Art by Joanna Kirk, Sebastien de Ganay, and Ena
Swansea. ($10)

ISSUE # 11 — OPEN CITY

Equivocal Landscape
Sam Brumbaugh, author of *Goodbye, Goodness*, debuts with
a story set in Kenya, Daphne Beal and Swamiji, Paula Bomer
sees red on a plane, Heather Larimer hits a dog, and Hunter
Kennedy on the sexual possibilities of Charlottesville versus
West Texas. Ford Madox Ford on the end of fun. Poetry by
Jill Bialosky and Rachel Wetzsteon. Art by Miranda
Lichtenstein and Pieter Schoolwerth; a love scene by Toru
Hayashi. Mungo Thomson passes notes. ($10)

ISSUE # 12 — OPEN CITY

Something Like Ten Million
The defacto life and death issue. Amazing debut stories
from Nico Baumbach, Michiko Okubo, and Sarah Porter;
Craig Chester writes on why he has the face he deserves;
a bushy, funny, and phallic art project from Louise
Belcourt. Special poetry section guest edited by Lee Ann
Brown. A photo essay of fleeing Manhattanites by Ken
Schles. The cover is beautiful and weird, a bright hole in
downtown Manhattan. ($10)

ISSUE # 14 — OPEN CITY

That Russian Question
Another excerpt from Amine Wefali's *Westchester
Burning (see Open City #8)*. Alicia Erian in *Jeopardy*.
Jocko Weyland does handplants for an audience of elk.
James Lasdun on travel and infidelity. Lara Vapnyar's
debut publication. Poetry by Steve Healy, Daniel Nester,
Lev Rubinshtein, and Daniel Greene. ($10)

ISSUE # 15 — OPEN CITY

I wait, I wait.
A brilliant outtake from Robert Bingham's *Lightning on the
Sun*. Ryan Kenealy on the girl who ran off with the circus;
Nick Tosches on Proust. Art by Allen Ruppersberg, David
Bunn, Nina Katchadourian, Matthew Higgs, and Matthew
Brannon. Stories by Evan Harris, Lewis Robinson, Michael
Sledge, and Bruce Jay Friedman. Rick Rofihe feels
Marlene. Poetry by Dana Goodyear, Nathaniel Bellows, and
Kevin Young. ($10)

ISSUE # 16 — OPEN CITY — I MARRIED AN ARTIST

Please send a check or
money order payable to:

Open City, Inc.
270 Lafayette Street, Suite 1412
New York, NY 10012

For credit-card orders, see www.opencity.org.

They're at it again.
Lara Vapnyar's "There Are Jews in My House," Chuck Kinder on Dagmar. Special poetry section guest edited by Honor Moore, including C. K. Williams, Victoria Redel, Eamon Grennan, and Carolyn Forché. Art by Stu Mead, Christoph Heemann, Jason Fox, Herzog film star Bruno S., and Sophie Toulouse, whose "Sexy Clowns" project has become a "character note for [our] intentions" (says the *Literary Magazine Review*). See what all the fuss is about. ($10)

I Want to Be Your Shoebox
Susan Chamandy on Hannibal's elephants and hockey, Mike Newirth's noirish "Semiprecious." Rachel Blake's "Elephants" (an unintentional elephant theme emerges). Poetry by Catherine Bowman and Rodney Jack. Art by Viggo Mortensen, Alix Lambert, Marcellus Hall, Mark Solotroff, and Alaskan Pipeline polar bear cover by Jason Middlebrook (we're still trying to figure out what the bear had for lunch). ($10)

Post Hoc Ergo Propter Hoc
Stories by Jason Brown, Bryan Charles, Amber Dermont, Luis Jaramillo, Dawn Raffel, Bryan Charles, Nina Shope, and Alicia Erian. Robert Olen Butler's severed heads. Poetry by Jim Harrison, Sarah Gorham, Trevor Dannatt, Matthew Rohrer & Joshua Beckman, and Harvey Shapiro. Art by Bill Adams, Juliana Ellman, Sally Ross, and George Rush. Eerie, illustrated children's story by Rick Rofihe and Thomas Roberston. Saucy cover by Wayne Gonzales. ($10)

Homecoming
"The Egg Man" a novella by Scott Smith, author of *A Simple Plan* (screenplay and book); Ryan Kenealy does God's math; an unpublished essay by Paul Bowles. Stories by Rachel Sherman, Sam Shaw, and Maxine Swann. Art by Shelter Serra and William McCurtin (of *Story of My Scab* and *Elk* fame). Poems by Anthony Roberts, Honor Moore, and David Lehman. ($10)

Ballast
Matthew Zapruder's "The Pajamaist," David Nutt's "Melancholera," fiction by Rachel Sherman, a Nick Tosches poem, Phillip Lopate's "Tea at the Plaza," David A. Fitschen on life on tour as a roadie. Poetry by Matt Miller and Alex Phillips. Art by Molly Smith, Robert Selwyn, Miranda Lichtenstein, Lorenzo Petrantoni, Billy Malone, and M Blash. ($10)

OPEN CITY

back issues

Fiction/Nonfiction
A special double-sided issue featuring fiction by Sam Lipsyte, Jerry Stahl, Herbert Gold, Leni Zumas, Matthew Kirby, Jonathan Baumbach, Ann Hillesland, Manuel Gonzales, and Leland Pitts-Gonzales. Nonfiction by Priscilla Becker, Vestal McIntyre, Eric Pape, Jocko Weyland, and Vince Passaro. ($10)

Prose by Poets
Prose and poetry by Anne Sexton, Nick Flynn, Jim Harrison, Wayne Koestenbaum, Joe Wenderoth, Glyn Maxwell, Rebecca Wolff, Vijay Seshadri, Jerome Badanes, Deborah Garrison, Jill Bialosky, Cynthia Kraman, Max Blagg, Thorpe Moeckel, Greg Purcell, Rodney Jack, Hadara Bar-Nadav, and Nancy Willard. ($10)

Secret Engines
Three debuts: Malerie Willens, Gerard Coletta, and Ian Martin. Stanley Moss as a bronze satyr; heavy breathing with Jeff Johnson. Stories by Jonathan Baumbach, Erin Brown, Wayne Conti, James Hannaham, and Claire Keegan. Poetry by Mark Hartenbach, Alex Lemon, and Baron Wormser. Art by Amy Bird, Jay Batlle, Noelle Tan, and Doug Shaeffer. ($10)

High Wire
Robert Stone's epic novella (set midway between the reigns of Elvis Presley and Bill Clinton); stories by Jonathan Ames, Charles Bukowski, Rivka Galchen, Jon Groebner, Said Shirazi, Giuseppe O. Longo, and Sarah Gardner Borden. Poetry by Howard Altmann, Jennifer Richter, and Ben Carlton Turner. Art by Ellen Harvey, Michael Scoggins, Mark C, and Duncan Hannah. ($10)

The New Soft Shoe
Brad Gooch on Flannery O'Connor at Iowa; stories by Kirsty Gunn, Mohammed Naseehu Ali, Matthew Specktor, Caedra Scott-Flaherty, Henry Alcalay, and Chris Spain. Poetry by Priscilla Becker, William Benton, John Fandel, Christopher Kang, Strawberry Saroyan, and Elizabeth Schmidt. Stunning collage cover by Balint Zsako. ($10)

"Matthew Specktor's

That Summertime Sound isn't so much a book as it is

a door, hinged in memory, and swinging wide to every

tenderhearted throb of lust and longing and precocious

regret still there where you left it, at the periphery of

adulthood. How does the novel perform this trick? By

prose as lucid and classical as Graham Greene's in *The*

End of the Affair, yet saturated in detail such that if you'd

never had the luck to outgrow an '80s teenage dream in

Columbus, Ohio, you'll feel you had after reading it."

                                        -- Jonathan Lethem

Late in Life

Vestal McIntyre

ACORNS POPPED UNDER THE TIRES OF CANDICE'S CAR AS IT wound through the leaf-canopied streets of outer Queens. When she reached the Long Island Expressway, traffic was moving more smoothly than she had expected. One o'clock was still early, even on a late-August Friday when everyone was headed out to the Hamptons.

"You took a half-day off for this?" Annie asked.

"I called in a favor," Candice replied with a flick of her head. A stranger would think that this and her other pet gesture, a wave of her hand over one eye, were neurotic tics. But those who knew her recognized that they were left over from when she had long, wavy hair that was always falling in her face. Or maybe they *were* neurotic tics that had just been laid bare by the cutting of her hair, like the bones of her long neck that had been made visible by the sinking of her skin. She was approaching fifty. Still, her skin was fresh and her jaw strong. A challenging kind of beauty remained in her large-featured face, even when it confronted you squarely as a road sign, as it tended to do.

"Well, I appreciate it," Annie said.

Candice gave another head-flick, this one accompanied by a shrug of her shoulder. "No biggie. I wouldn't want some new friend to take you, or some student. Someone who didn't know Sarah."

"*Well*—" Annie said, but didn't go on. They both knew that it wouldn't have come to that. Annie had many friends old and new to drive her places since her license had been revoked after a series of fender benders.

They were quiet as the neighborhoods on either side of the expressway gave way to walls of green, and overpasses became less frequent.

"Are you still seeing that fellow, James?" Annie asked.

"Your memory is starting to go. No. Not for a year."

After a pause, Annie asked, "How are Joan and the others?"

"Fine, fine," Candice said airily. Then she caught herself. "No, they're not. They're all getting dogs. Every time we plan something, someone has to cancel because her dog is barfing on the rug. Susan actually brought hers to tai chi! She leashed it to a tree, and it paced and whined all class long. In the corner of my eye I could see Susan waving at it from Repulse Monkey position."

"Upward-facing Dog," Annie offered.

Candice patted her hand. "That's yoga, dear. I've told them all, my house is a canine-free zone. If you want to stay home teaching Sparky where to poop instead of coming over for lunch, then fine. I hope the conversation's as good."

"Dogmatic."

"I swear, I want to round them all up and put them all to sleep."

"The dogs or the gals?"

"The dogs. Why not? I don't love them. Is there a law that you have to love every dog?"

"No, but you can't blame the poor animals if your luncheons aren't what they used to be."

"Who can I blame, then? You?"

The old Annie would have volleyed that one back. Together they would have built it into something crowned by laughter. But she had become feeble. Her best feature had always been her big eyes that seemed to implore to be understood, especially when she was explaining an idea. This made her students feel like they could save her just by nodding. But several years ago she had stopped wearing contacts, and the thick glasses she wore instead not only shrunk those eyes but crowded into the lens warped funhouse figures from the world behind her. Annie now blinked those miniaturized eyes at Candice. Her mild smile didn't falter, but her head turned to gaze out the window.

An hour later, they took an exit and passed through a small town into the countryside. Out here, Long Island held onto its last bit of charm. Fields here were still used to grow crops, mailboxes were cloaked in climbing flowers, clusters of sleek-coated horses turned their heads in unison to watch the car pass. The old fence posts that ran along the road listed this way and that, held up, it seemed, only by the wire that ran between them. "Left up here . . ." Annie quietly directed, "Now right." In a hollow, thick trees threw a night-like shadow over the road. Then they retreated, and it was day again. "Up here on the right. This is it."

"Here? This looks like any other spot."

"See where people park?" There was a flat area at the side of the road where broken glass glinted in the weeds. "The path starts there," Annie said, indicating a gap in a mossy, vine-strewn stone wall.

Candice pulled over and killed the engine. Flicking her head and pushing back her phantom bangs, she asked, "Do you need help?"

"No, no. I've gone down this path a hundred times." She hoisted herself out of the car and took a shopping bag from where it sat wedged between the two overnight bags.

Candice was suddenly flustered. "Are you sure? I could help you partway down, then wait."

"Nope," Annie said with a practiced kind of cheer. "I'll be back. Half hour at most." Holding the bag high out of reach of the weeds, she waddled toward the gap in the wall.

Annie had always been stocky and a little crooked in the hip and shoulder. The extent of her daily exercise was a five-minute walk to the subway. It had never been beauty or grace that made women love her. But now as she disappeared around the bushes, she seemed even denser than before, heavy in the step, as if during those endless hours in the study all her weight had settled into her feet.

Using buttons on the door handle, Candice opened all the windows. It was cooler here than in Brooklyn, and there was a pleasant

3

nutty flavor to the air. Wind stirred the tops of the trees, and the insects' drone ebbed and flowed. She took out her book, knowing she would only read a page or two before she fell asleep. Lithium. In the past three years it had done her a great service, but it had robbed her of her chief pleasure, reading under the afternoon sun. Despite her doctor's claim that it would have few side effects, sleep now waited in every gap in her day.

All her adult life, Candice had turned down therapists who suggested she try a mood stabilizer. The problem wasn't in her brain. The problem was in the world, which was run by good-old boys who used religion to trick everyone else into maintaining the status quo—tilling the fields, putting dinner on the table every night in the hope of a reward in heaven. Wasn't that what she and her generation had been arguing in all those chants and folk songs? Must she now give in and take a pill to reconcile herself with this world? Was part of growing old betraying your younger self?

She did suffer, though, more than was fair. At last, she had given lithium a test run, and it had worked.

Even now she would never submit to Prozac or Zoloft or any of those other pills that had turned her friends into happy monsters. But lithium was just a salt. A salt that reined in her rampages and softened her falls.

Candice was awakened when Annie sat heavily into the seat, mopping her forehead with a handkerchief and struggling to catch her breath.

"What happened?" Candice cried.

"Had a bit of a tumble on the hillside."

Candice took the shopping bag, which was torn, from Annie and put it in the backseat. The box inside had been emptied and flattened.

"I should have helped you, Annie. Look at you! You're covered in dust." Candice began patting down her shirt, raising a white cloud. Then she froze. "It's not—"

"No," said Annie, "just dirt. I had already scattered the ashes when I fell."

Candice swallowed and continued dusting her off, a little less vigorously now.

"Some water would be nice," Annie said.

Candice handed her the bottle and started the car, to get the air conditioner going. Annie drank, then let her head fall back against the headrest. After a minute, she sat up and said, "All better, captain."

Candice started to say something, to chide her, but found that her throat was constricted. This was how far Annie had come. It was time for a cane, maybe an I've-fallen-and-I-can't-get-up alert button. A Craftmatic adjustable bed, a "Clapper." They had made fun of the commercials together, quoting the velvet-voiced welcomes to old age—*Just look at what your AARP membership gets you*—and now Annie had gone and reached it. Candice drove, focusing on pretty aspects of the countryside until the lump in her throat went down. Then she started afresh: "So, where did that path go?"

The words burst out of Annie as if she had been hoping to be asked: "A fishing hole. We used to fish there. There's the biggest weeping willow you've ever seen. Its branches kind of lash the water's surface, gently. You can watch it for hours. You don't catch much, but it's a lovely place to spend a day."

"It sounds beautiful."

"I can take you if you'd like."

"Don't be silly. It's your and Sarah's place. We have our own places."

Annie poked her thigh. "Café Loup."

Candice took her hand and squeezed it.

Annie had taken Candice to this cavern of a restaurant on Thirteenth Street after class one evening, and that was the start of their affair. Annie was a literature professor and Candice an adult student, a divorcée slowly meandering toward a master's degree. Annie didn't mention on that first dinner that she had a lover at home. Later, when they lived together, Candice would come in from Brooklyn at the end of the day and meet Annie at Café Loup. On the long banquette, editors sat next to their authors and spread manuscripts among dishes and wine glasses. This was the New York Annie had fought her way east to find many years before, one Candice had never imagined growing up in Sheepshead Bay. Once, they had been seated near Allen Ginsberg, and what followed must have been the quietest dinner of their life together. Usually they sparred and joked and talked over each other, but now they said very little, hoping to catch a few words from the poet and his companions. Annie had taught "Howl" for years in her Literature of Protest class. She had taught it to Candice.

Annie didn't take back her hand, and neither did Candice. The sun grew red and touched the mottled black line of the treetops in the distance. When they reached the inn and walked into the restaurant, Annie had a noticeable limp.

"You hurt your leg in the fall," Candice said.

"Might have twisted my ankle a bit."

"We'll have to ice it."

"Ice will do the trick. It'll be better by morning."

They ate under a sloped, stuccoed ceiling with exposed beams in the little four-table restaurant. There were plug-in fountains humming and bubbling in every nook. After dinner they went to the adjoining office where a teenaged girl checked them in. She had golden skin and black curly hair and wore jeans that rode so low Candice could see where the curve of her belly began to flatten. *The innkeeper's daughter,* mused Candice. *She spends her evenings here, a summer job. Daytime, she's all coconut-oiled up on her towel, with boys lined up all the way down the beach.* For a second Candice ached for those summers of necking with boys in the woods just out of reach of the campfire's unsteady amber light. The crackling logs would collapse, and she'd pull away to watch the crazily swirling sparks rise like demons into the night.

"We have you in rooms four and five upstairs," the girl said. "The bathroom's in the hall."

"Two rooms?" Candice said.

The girl flinched.

"Annie, you're being ridiculous." She turned her face back on the girl. "We'll only be needing one room."

The girl looked to Annie, who shrugged.

"I swear, Annie," Candice said as she trudged up the narrow staircase behind her, carrying both suitcases, "two rooms. What a waste of money!"

"Just wanted to do what's appropriate."

"For a radical, you're such a fuddy-duddy. How many years did we share a bed? Really, Annie, this late in life you should be more worried about what's left in your bank account than what's *appropriate*."

In the middle of the night, Candice rose and crept down the hall to pee. Then she returned, shut the door behind her, and stood for a while to let her eyes adjust. Annie lay as if in state, with her arms at her sides on top of the blanket. She had always been such a neat sleeper. During spells of insomnia, Candice would sometimes watch her, and feelings of adoration would turn to panic. She wasn't breathing! She'd shake her, and those eyes would open and implore, and Candice would be caught—crazy again.

Now she lay beside her and copied her so they were like twin Lenins laid out in Red Square. It wasn't comfortable to sleep this way. How did Annie do it? Candice took her hand and felt Annie apply a gentle pressure. This made her sleep seem even more like wakefulness, like she was faking it, writing books in her mind as she waited for morning.

Candice woke in the morning feeling an unnamable, unreasonable anger. She returned from a shower to find Annie sitting on the bed, waiting her turn.

"You look like a little old lady," Candice said. "All you need is some pigeons at your feet."

"I am a little old lady. I'm little, old, and a *lady*." Annie moved to rise.

"Hold it. I want to look at that ankle." Candice held Annie's legs in either hand. The taut, speckled skin was veined with blue like Roquefort cheese. While one ankle showed a little through the puffy flesh, the other didn't. "It's swollen. You probably have a sprain. We'll have to ice it in the car. So much for our walk on the beach. We'd better just head back. I have things to do around the house anyway."

Annie sighed. "I suppose I should get back to writing, myself." Then she shuffled into the hall, leaving Candice to stew. Of course Annie didn't insist. A walk on the beach meant nothing to her.

They drove. At one point Annie said, timidly, "You miss your hair."

"Why do you say that?"

"You still push it out of your face, even though it's not there."

"I don't."

"You do."

"Well, why wouldn't I? I do miss it. When I still had my hair, young men would ask me to dance. Ask Joan. There was one she called Tarzan who kept sending me drinks at the bar, and that was just— what?—three years ago. He couldn't have been over thirty-five. Big and handsome."

"Then why don't you grow it back?"

Candice toyed with the idea of telling her that the lithium had made it thin, to see her eyes turn contrite. "Because I'm getting old, Annie, and I don't want to be some gray, frizzy ex-hippy. Maybe if I moved to Vermont or Sedona, but not here."

"You may be getting old, Candice, but you'll always be younger than me."

"Is that supposed to make me feel better? Well, it doesn't. We were going to have a beautiful day on the beach, but instead you hurt your-self and brought up my thinning hair."

"I don't want to fight, Candice."

"Of course you don't. You never did. You wanted me to do the fight-ing, while you sat there like some sort of angel or patient mother or something. *Oh no*, to join in the fight would make *me* seem less of a nut. Then we would just be a couple arguing the way couples do. But this way you get to play the saint while I'm the hysteric. Yes, just like that, bow your head like I'm going to beat on you. Do you know what an antifeminist thing that is to do? To put another woman in the position of the hysteric. I can't believe you get to teach that stuff. Do you still use feminism in your classes? Honest to God, you shouldn't be allowed. *You* telling young girls about feminism. *The idea*. You clearly value men over women; you act like one."

Annie sat stiffly watching the road ahead. Sometimes Candice's rage spent itself quickly like a roman candle, and a docile comment offered five minutes later would elicit a docile answer. But not this time. An ember remained.

"I'm going to write the department a letter. It really is my responsibility. I should have done it years ago. The fact that I haven't makes me complicit, in a way. They should know what a hypocrite you are, using feminism in your classes when you manipulate other women this way, forcing us into these old-fashioned roles. Only *you* do this to me, Annie. All the men treated me with respect."

Candice could feel Annie aching to be rid of her, longing for her books in her dim study with its French doors onto the garden, unopenable because they had been bound with vines. What a fitting metaphor. Sarah had humored her wishes to let the vines grow— gentle Sarah. She was so perfectly accommodating that she hadn't even cut them during the years Annie lived with Candice.

"Did you do it to Sarah? Did you drive her to fits?" Candice asked. "I know you didn't before me. You said yourself, your house was quiet as a chapel. But after me? Did you practice the tricks you had invented on me in the meantime?"

Annie inhaled as if to speak, then let out a long, rattling exhale.

After a few minutes, Candice removed her foot from the gas pedal. It took a while for the car to slow, and when Annie noticed, she made a little jump. *That jump.* She said nothing, but now one shoulder rode a little closer to that ear. Weeds made a gentle hiss against the car side as Candice pulled onto the shoulder and stopped. She swiveled to face Annie.

"I want you to answer me. I always let questions go unanswered, but I feel like I owe this one to Sarah. Did you drive her to fits and sit there watching quietly?"

"For Christ's sake, Candice, *stop it.*"

Candice recoiled. Annie's responses were always so embarrassing, somehow—so abject and real. Why was that? Candice's own anger was, to her own ear, elegant and rhythmic, like Beethoven. Annie's was like something hacked up from the bottom of her lungs.

Candice settled back to wait. To the left of the road lay miles of marsh leading to the Great South Bay. The grasses dipped their fuzzy heads in the sea breeze and cast a rippling border onto the road. To the right, a brush-covered slope led up to a forested hill. Everywhere, tiny gray moths flitted into the air then back into the brush. It was like a paper fight was going on down there. No cars passed. This used to be a busy road before they built the expressway. Candice considered stating her demand again, to let Annie know that she would not drive on until she and Sarah were paid this respect. Annie could be so selfish and small, the way she sat squinting at the road. In her mind she was probably already back in her study. Candice shook her head, adjusted her seat, sighed loudly.

With a bold step of its backward-bending, powder-blue leg, a bird emerged from the marsh and into the road. Candice gasped when she saw it. Annie looked over and said "Oh!" with delight. The bird's narrow beak, black and shiny as its eye, curved up at the end, like an ice pick which had been bent by hard use. Its head and body bobbed with a grace that contrasted with its jerky footsteps. There was something human in this contrast. The foot poised with its long toes hanging like a handkerchief before being splayed again on the asphalt. Hang, *splay* . . . hang, *splay* . . . went the feet. Each step comprised alternating gestures: demure, *obscene* . . . tentative, *overt* . . . dangle, *splat* . . . dangle, *splat*. Candice had never seen this kind of bird before. It crossed the border, and the sunlight revealed its head to be not gray, as it had appeared in shadow, but a rich rusty red with a white ring around the eye. "What is it?" Candice wondered aloud.

"An avocet. An American avocet. I've never seen one this close. We'd get them in the back field when we flood irrigated."

"The back field?" For a moment Candice thought she meant the backyard—hers and Sarah's.

"In Utah. Growing up."

"Ah." Sometimes she forgot that Annie had grown up in the fields out west. It explained some of her rough-edged naïveté. She could endlessly explore the subtleties of literature, but had a farmer's love of the concrete when it came to her own emotions. With a tug of sympathy, Candice remembered how she had to tie all the bows at Christmastime—even on her own presents—since Annie's fingers were too big and blunt.

The avocet, which was passing close by before disappearing behind the hood of the car, tilted its head to eye Candice, then blinked. A white lid came up from below to cover the onyx bead. It was less like the drawing down of a curtain—as humans did over their eyes—and more like the pulling up of wrinkled trousers.

Backwards knees, upside-down eyes. Candice emitted a little chuckle of wonderment. She lifted herself to see that the bird had safely entered the brush, then she started up the car. She would let Annie off the hook. If she was really going to get any housework done today, it was getting late.

By the time they reached Annie's house, Candice felt only a hangover of anger, as pressure behind her eyes. She pinched the bridge of her nose as she came around the car to where Annie stood with suitcase in hand.

"Thanks, Candice," she said. "And sorry about all that at the end."

With a toss of her head Candice made it clear that it was best left alone. "I'll come in with you," she said. "I want to take another look at that ankle."

"No. It's fine."

"You always want everything to be fine. You're clearly injured."

"I'm fine."

"You need to put it up."

"Look." Annie did a circus tightrope walk up the path, holding her suitcase out as a balance, twirled, and walked back. "See?"

Candice's giggles quickly turned to sobs. "I worry about you. You're all alone in that house with all those stairs. What if you fall and break a hip? That's always the beginning of the end, the broken hip. It's silly for you to be alone. Maybe it's time, right? For you to come back?"

Annie put down the suitcase, drew near, and looked up into Candice's face. "Kind of late in life to be starting again, don't you think?"

"Why?" Candice demanded. *You did with her*, was her unspoken thought.

Annie took her by her shoulders. Candice tucked her chin, but her hair wasn't there anymore to hide her tears. Annie petted Candice's arms a few times, then took her face in her hands and gave her a tender smile.

"I hate these," Candice said, removing the glasses. Annie *did* love her—it was there in her eyes; she just couldn't take her. She had lived too long in peace and quiet to trade it again for fights and noise and laughter.

I should have left Sarah alone, Candice thought. The plan had been to selflessly drive Annie out, wait while she spread the ashes, then comfort her over dinner, all without mentioning the dead wife's name. But Candice always broke her own rules.

Back when they lived together, Candice had spent a winter doing research for Annie's book on George Eliot. When it was released, Annie toasted her at a department dinner: "To Candice. She wrote the damn book, you know."

As Candice blushed at all the applause and grinning faces, a voice inside her said, *You can never say what she said—that you wrote this book.* But of course she had, again and again. As soon as she had a few cocktails in her at any party, she'd tell some handsome student, "I wrote the Eliot book, you know. Annie just put her name on it." And in arguments, while the author herself sat silent with averted eyes: "That's my goddamn book. You said yourself I wrote it."

I didn't write it. She now silently flogged herself with the truth. *I didn't write it. You wrote it.*

Annie kissed her on either cheek. In an utterly kind voice free of any irony, she said, "Find yourself another Tarzan." She took back her glasses, put them on, and went into the house, leaving her suitcase on the sidewalk.

Candice stood for a while, arms folded, waiting to greet Annie with a victorious expression when she came back out.

When Candice and Annie had been together nearly ten years, Sarah, that old lover who Annie had left at home while she took Candice to Café Loup, underwent a mastectomy. Annie started dropping by Sarah's house—this house—with groceries. When the cancer returned, she took her to appointments. Then Candice came home from work one day to find Annie packing her things. "It's better this way," she said.

Candice baited her to add, *I owe it to her,* or, *I'll come back after she's dead.* But, of course, she wouldn't. She was too kind.

No, Candice now said, *she wasn't being kind. She didn't owe her. She loved her!* It felt good to slap herself around like this. *I am unendurable. No wonder they're all getting dogs.*

At the beginning, Annie would go to Brooklyn once or twice a week and Candice would make dinner. Annie would let off steam about the endless chemotherapy appointments and Sarah's failing mental focus. They would have sex in the urgent, wrestling way they always had, then Annie would come back here to sleep at Sarah's side.

One night, Candice put her foot down. "You're treating me like your concubine," she said.

Annie acquiesced, as she always did. "Right, absolutely. I'm being horrible. We can't do this anymore."

What a fool Candice had been, throwing back that last precious bit of love! She had assumed that Annie would come back once Sarah was gone. Or, when that failed, once her grief had faded. Or, when that failed, once she had spread the ashes.

She didn't owe her. She loved her.

The masochistic thrill of facing facts faded, and Annie still hadn't reemerged from the house. Candice had half a mind to leave the suitcase here on the sidewalk to be stolen. Or, better yet, to be returned by a concerned neighbor who regarded Annie as a doddering old granny. In her embarrassment, Annie would see that Candice had been right. It *was* time. She *did* need her.

But Candice decided to take the high road. She took the suitcase and put it just inside the front door. As expected, Annie had already closed herself in the study.

Now righteous, Candice was able to put a new spin on things as she drove home. How condescending it had been of Annie to pat her on the head like that! *Go find yourself another Tarzan.* As if men were a dime a dozen. Annie had recently told her that she was envious—*envious*—that Candice could sleep with both women and men. "It gives you twice the options," she had said, unaware of how callow and insulting and *cruel* a thing this was to say. Annie had always acted as if everything you needed from life was there on a banquet table, and all you had to do was fill your plate. Always the optimist. Love would be served up again and again in endless courses, all you could eat.

Well, for her it *was* that way; she was born with that kind of heart. So she could afford to sit there, sated and smug.

Now Candice sat parked in front of the brownstone, one floor of which was hers alone. Geraniums in the window boxes. Curlicued wrought iron. It would take the strength of hundreds to get her up those stairs.

Annie would not have been envious if she knew the truth. Candice had to push and fight. Life had not offered her endless servings of love. Only one.

Parallel

Billy Collins

An undernourished horse
harnessed with leather
to a sled of dead weight—

a poem straining to be poetry,
its ribs visible beneath the whip
of the master of fine arts.

Simile

When he told me he expected me to pay for dinner,
I was like give me a break.

I was not the exact equivalent of give me a break.
I was just similar to give me a break.

As I said, I was like give me a break.

I would like to tell you
how I managed to approximate give me a break
without being identical to give me a break,

but all I can come up with
is that I was aware of a certain similarity
between me and give me a break.

And that was enough for me
at that point in the evening

even if it meant I would fall short
of standing up from the table and screaming
give me a break,

for God's sake will you please give me a break?

No, for that moment
with the rain streaking the restaurant windows
and the waiter approaching,

the most I felt I could be was like,
to a certain degree,

give me a break.

Thank-You Notes

With my mother looking over my shoulder
I thanked my uncle Gerry
in my very best penmanship for the tie

and Helen for the pistol and holster
and someone for the winter gloves,

but now I am writing other notes
at a small cherry desk by an open window
with the sun and breeze coming in,

to thank everyone I saw today
on my long walk to the post office

and anyone who ever gave me directions
or placed a hand on my shoulder,
or cut my hair or fixed my car,

and while I am at it,
thanks to everyone who happened to die
on the same day that I was born.

Thank you for stepping aside to make room for me,
for giving up your seat,
getting out of the way, to be blunt.

Billy Collins

I waited until almost midnight
on that day in March before I appeared,
all slimy and squinting, in order to leave time

for enough of the living
to drive off a bridge or collapse in a hallway
so that I could enter without causing a stir.

I am writing now to thank everyone
who drifted off that day
like smoke from a row of blown-out candles—
for giving up your only flame.

One day, I will follow your example
by stepping politely out of the path
of an oncoming infant, but not today

with the subtropical sun warming this page
and the wind stirring the fronds in the palmettos,

and me about to begin another note
on my very best stationery
to the ones who are making room right now

for the daily host of babies,
descending like bees with their wings and stingers,
ready to get busy with all their earthly joys and tasks.

Pleasure

Eva Marer

MIMI AND CHARLOTTE CREPT TO THE TOP OF THE STAIRS AND peered over the landing at their father. They giggled and hushed each other, spying on him in the kitchen, as he struggled to fish hot banana peppers from their jar with a dessert fork.

István always took his breakfast standing, like a horse, straight from the Formica countertop. He was naked, except for a pair of sagging underwear and his wooden leg, still dressed in last night's black sock and business shoe from his meeting with the Soviet delegation. Though he was an ardent enemy of the Soviet Union, István wore a Lenin-style beard, de rigueur for an economist specializing in arcane Eastern European themes in a Midwest college town. Mimi and Charlotte had secret paroxysms of delight, watching their father swing about on his one hairy foot, unmindful of the well-dressed leg.

Today was Saturday and Mimi and Charlotte could play all day. They were perfectly dressed for a day of amusement in periwinkle star-studded briefs. Unlike their father, they would not work all day in their underwear, but take turns dressing in their mother's gowns and shoes. They each clutched a tiny, corduroy animal: an elephant and a lion. Graciously they allowed the animals to peer over the landing, and the animals laughed too.

With the beasts, they made four KGB agents. Mimi knew that István was only an assistant professor, but he had quite a reputation

in the Eastern bloc, where he was considered one of the 'Slav Seven.'
He told Mimi that his papers were routinely smuggled into Warsaw,
Moscow, and East Berlin, to the peril of those who carried them. His
work on exchange rates had even brought him to testify before the
World Bank and Congress. "He's hiding the currency conversibility
chart in the hollow leg," Mimi whispered.

"Convertibility," Charlotte corrected. She refused to be KGB on
principle, and would only be CIA or Interpol. Mimi played along but
secretly she knew herself to be a double agent.

Of all the games, Mimi liked best to play alone with her father. She
accompanied him to international conferences, where she sat quietly,
taking notes in colored pencil. They took baths together (he wore his
soggy underwear, of course) and slept in his bed when her mother
allowed it. He told her bedtime stories of the evil Doctor Mengele,
wielding his baton at the gates of Auschwitz. In questionable cases,
István said, the doctor examined your hands to see if they were rough
or smooth. The doctor had no use for silky-pawed intellectuals. Mimi
said she would have rubbed her hands in gravel to outsmart him, but
István only smiled a distant, wistful smile and changed the subject.
He told how he had lost his leg to an infection in the Budapest ghet-
to, where there wasn't any medicine, and wasn't it lucky that one of
the old Jews was a surgeon and had the wherewithal to sterilize a gap-
toothed saw and hack off the limb before gangrene set in. "If not for
that old man, I would not have survived the war, *Butzik*," he said in
his voice of ceaseless wonder. Mimi clapped her hands and said,
"More, more!" He had many such entries for the "If … Then" game.
"If Nagymama had not been such a *kutya*," he would say of Mimi's
grandmother, "I would never have come to America." He said, "If the
war had gone on just one more month, I would have been gassed
with the rest, and you would never have been born." Mimi delighted
in the syntax and repetition of such sentences, though they frightened her with their finality. "I was just a child then," he would say,
preempting himself from blame.

For breakfast, István ate whatever they'd had for dinner the previous night, usually chicken soup or chicken *paprikás* or potato
paprikás or pork *paprikás* or spicy *léscó*. Mimi's mother Gertrud had

learned how to cook Hungarian food from István's cousin Káta when she married him, and evenings their dinner table burned a fiery red. Some nights she made steak and salad or hamburgers on the grill, because she couldn't expect her children to eat red food *every* night. István always ate his own crimson leftovers straight from the pot.

Mimi and Charlotte liked to watch their father pivot and fly on his well-heeled leg, but they preferred not to watch him eat. He conversed with his food in a greasy language that made them uneasy. He sucked the marrow clean from every chicken bone and sometimes even moaned and cooed into his soup as though he saw faint interlocutors to be appeased there.

Mimi's mother had her own problems with food, but unlike István, she tried to keep them secret. Gertrud skimmed the fat off the top of the chicken soup and stored it in a jar they all knew she hid behind the ketchup bottle in the refrigerator door, and secretly spread on black bread, and dusted with salt and pepper, in the middle of the night.

"It's memory food," Gertrud would say if she were caught. She said it apologetically—for she was not supposed to have quirks like their father. She did not eat standing up but neatly at the table with her plump forearms balanced on the edge of the table and her arms spread out like wings. She was chastened when they caught her in the act, a heathen chorus of American children.

"Puke!"

"Grody!"

"Gross!"

Such was the opinion of schmaltz in their house.

Gertrud turned her high-fat snack into a moral lesson. "During the war, we had no milk or butter, you know even the Germans suffered too." Both she and István had been children then, and blameless, she reminded them.

Gertrud was a Lutheran and made the children go to Sunday school even on days they didn't want to, but she was not a Jesus-thumper. "God is music," she would say, "and the Lutherans have the best music." By that she meant Bach, of course, and even their father listened to Bach, so he must believe in God too, though he never spoke of it.

Luckily Gertrud had been called to an emergency session of the church council, and had put their sister Olive, who was ten years older than Mimi, in charge. Olive took her responsibilities remotely, that is from a recliner in the basement. And so Mimi and Charlotte had been amusing themselves all day, sneaking into the secret crevices of the house where useful tools of pleasure might lurk, such as the wooden hammer they rode like a horse, or the plastic dry-cleaning bags in the garage on which they stamped impressions of their faces by a mere intake of breath.

The house held many rooms, and in each room lurked objects of pleasure. Sometimes they foraged into István's chest of drawers, and pulled out all the stump socks, and sang the "Stump Sock" song and marched around the house with the socks pulled over their heads. The stump socks were quite useful for games, because they could be made to hold toys: who carried the most won. No one reprimanded them, but the stump socks were frequently whisked away, even if, for example, they constituted the moat of a castle. Their disappearance gave the socks more value, for Mimi and Charlotte never knew when they would vanish.

When they played "little people" with the Fisher Price school-house, Mimi would secretly hide the orange schoolmaster in her frock and pull him out discreetly as though she'd won him fair and square: *Doc Mengele*. But Mimi doesn't tell it's the doctor, secretly she is guilty; also listen: her own hands would not pass the doctor's test, but in this instance, her tiny fist envelops him, swallowing his rank: *Doc Mengele!* She positions him on the jamb of the schoolhouse and has him speak roughly: girls to the left, boys to the right! The little children stream in columns through the door, taking their little-people seats in the one-room schoolhouse. He's supposed to be the principal seating them, but Mimi knows he's really Doc Mengele wielding his power of life-and-death. After the game, she grasps the toy to her lips and kisses and strokes him. "Doc Mengele," she whispers tenderly in his little-person ear.

Charlotte suggests they play "Upstairs, Downstairs," a game that requires them to slide down the carpeted staircase on their rumps. They did so now, clutching their corduroy animals. Halfway down the stairs, they came to the cold stone foyer. The storm clouds had parted and a shaft of sunlight angled through the transom. The light was fresh and dappled as it coursed through the high rain-beaded window. Mimi lay back, felt the hard step against her shoulder blades and the warm sun in her face. Charlotte looked at her quizzically, but maneuvered into the same position beside her, to see if there might be a game in this. Charlotte was almost two years older and much broader than Mimi, so the outlines of her body could not be fully enveloped by the sun, the same way she could not be fully in Papa's embrace, Mimi thought. Charlotte was her mother's child, and Mimi belonged to her father, though no one outright said so. When they went on rides at the fair, that's how they paired up, or in seats on trains or in airplanes, and no one questioned it. Mimi and Charlotte belonged to each other too, of course, a pair, the way they knew without speaking that if Charlotte's face were cut in half by shadow, Mimi too had to relinquish her place in the sun.

They slid the rest of the way down the stairs to the basement, ka-bunk, ka-bunk. They slunk behind the high-backed denim sofa to spy on their sister in her recliner. Olive usually ignored her little sisters, or sent them to fetch refills on her Cokes and Cheetohs. Sometimes, to impress her friends, she forced Mimi into a hatbox and stowed her on a high shelf in a closet so that everyone could marvel at her tiny stature. Sometimes she would take Mimi into the forest where the railroad tracks ran behind their house, and order her to lie between two railroad ties while she raced home to call her friends. Mimi felt flushed and frightened at such times, but important too, emerging, Houdini-like, to applause, demonstrating how she could suck in her gut and whittle herself down to almost nothing in the space between the rails. The train ran only twice a day, at dawn and at dusk, so Mimi knew she risked little in the daylight. Still, she was afraid of the train, the memory of its night whistle.

From behind the denim sofa, Mimi and Charlotte surveyed the scene. Olive was propped back in the recliner, twirling her unwashed hair, watching a *Star Trek* rerun on TV. She wore a metal contraption around her head that attached to her teeth and made her look futuristic and dangerous. At the rare high school football–games Mimi and Charlotte were permitted to attend, Olive wore a cheerleader jumper and shook pompoms at boys who stuffed their fists in their pockets and stared, and later she snuck under the bleachers and smoked sweet-smelling grass with long-haired types who could have been boys or girls, it was hard to tell. Now she wore her customary morose expression. Mimi knew for a fact that Olive stayed up late kissing with boys, listening to the newest tunes on the radio from the Band and the Byrds. Mimi liked the Beatles, but she particularly liked nursery rhymes sung in French, or the grand Mozart symphonies that made her father leap from his chair, transported to the realm of the sublime. "Mozart is the greatest composer who ever lived!" he shouted and Mimi clapped her hands.

These superlative moods sometimes overtook István—suddenly the world shifted and everything was the best he'd ever encountered—to the consternation of everyone but Mimi. In such moods, he could not be stopped. "That's the most amazing sports car I've ever seen!" he might say, as if he knew anything about cars. "It's the best Chinese restaurant in town," he would insist, though the others knew it to be only mediocre. He took pleasure in the fact that he had only to point at what the busboys were eating to get a special meal that was not on the menu. Above all, he liked the restaurant because it was subdued and spacious. István could not abide sudden loud noises of any kind, and above all hated to be cramped or jostled. At home, he gasped and flinched if one of his children so much as tapped on his study door. They had learned to make gentle warning noises before knocking, shuffling their feet in the hall, or clearing their throats, but even so, he was always startled. They would hear his scream and the rustle of papers fluttering to the floor, and open the door to find his hand on his heart and his face contorted with rage. "You cannot just . . ." he would start to shout, but his voice trailed off.

Once a tornado blew through town as was common in the Midwest, and Gertrud set about opening the windows.

"What are you doing?" István asked.

"István," she replied, with the lilt in her voice that warned him her nerves were frayed. "In a tornado, you open up the windows to alleviate the pressure. Otherwise the house might explode."

"Really? Really?" he said with a tone of great admiration for he imagined only his wife was aware of this obscure and remarkable fact.

Olive spotted Mimi behind the couch and threw a book at her, striking her on the head. Mimi screamed.

"Shut up, shut up!" Olive barked as the U.S.S. *Enterprise* returned from a commercial break.

István never ventured into the basement. "Too much like a bomb shelter," Olive sniggered. To get her attention, he stood on the landing and flung things over the railing, such as his daughters' shoes. Olive only laughed and threw her shoes back upstairs, striking him in the shin. "May your bitchy mother live to be seven hundred years old!" he swore in Hungarian. He didn't mean anything against their mother; that was just a standard Hungarian cuss.

"What a racket!" Olive complained, rolling her eyes at the whirl-squeak of the linoleum as István twirled heavy-footed overhead. She turned up the volume on the television.

To Mimi the sound of the leg was reassuring. She always knew it was her father coming to her room at night by the uneven creaking of the floorboards under the weight of his one bad leg. That was a soothing sound, the whimper of the ground beneath his feet. She knew he would stop by her room last, because she was his favorite, they all said so. Under the bronze bas-relief that her mother had hung above her bed—full of ominous purpose, the mournful Burghers of Calais, dignified in their disgrace, strode single file to deliver to the barbarians the keys to the gates of the city—István told her bedtime stories about the war, the revolution, about being a Jew. He drew vivid pictures of the evil images he had seen. He was not athletic or handy like some of her friends' fathers, was useless with firearms and tennis racquets, but he volleyed stories that sometimes made Mimi bolt upright in the middle of the night in a dead cold sweat. Other times his stories lulled her into a deep dreamless sleep. For Mimi, being with Papa meant pleasure—in horror and in peace.

Mimi and Charlotte crawled back up the stairs to see what István might do next. Mimi rubbed the corduroy ribs of her tiny stuffed elephant. Lately she had come into the startling awareness of her power over the elephant and occasionally smothered it against her chest. The pleasure she felt at bending the animal to her will was now tempered by a gruesome feeling. So she took care only to smother the animal long enough to teach it a lesson but not to kill it. This she was doing quietly even as she laughed with her sister.

It had recently occurred to Mimi that if she possessed this kind of authority over a mere corduroy elephant, she must enjoy a similar ascendancy over all her stuffed animals. Just yesterday she had picked up Teddy, outfitted in the little sweater Oma had knitted for him, and threw him to the ground in front of her mother's vanity mirror. She was possessed with punishing Teddy and rushed toward him blaring "Bad Teddy!" but at the very last second, instead of striking him, she scooped him up in her arms and ran headlong into the vanity mirror. She had changed her mind, and was cradling Teddy, unaware that she was sitting in a pile of glass shards, looking triumphant when her mother ran into the room. She was only triumphant because she had saved Teddy from her own wrath, and narrowly escaped a sin, and was covering his face in kisses.

Gertrud screamed and picked her out of the broken glass, looked for cuts, and then seemed to be angry when there were none. From her earliest years, whenever Mimi did something malicious, and then when a second even worse consequence rose out if it, she wondered, was she responsible only for the first bad thing or for the whole catastrophe? This was a complicated problem yet beyond her reckoning.

Drawings

Elliott Puckette

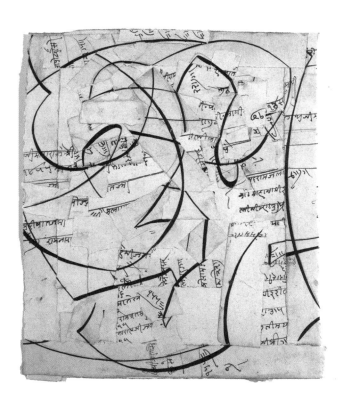

nir au bout
tes choses .
êtres devoit
née ; des figu...
précédoient ...

dal Abbat. Ridolf. Venet. sopra alcuni M...

des douze mille ans assignés
La destruction & la rénov...
se faire dans le Cercle qu'il...
...es que ceux qui en étoient...
chacune de ces révolutions ,

...nes de vie & de mœurs bien différentes , & ils assuroient... furent représentés par les...
leur temps étoient moins agréables aux Dieux , que ceux... eurent aussi des Minerves ,
...vécus avant eux. La plus grande partie de ces opinions , & les Furies mêmes furent...
celles des Phéniciens & des Égyptiens , passa aussi chez... recs ne donnerent guere qu'à...
qui Orphée les enseigna , & l'on les retrouve dans Ar... A Diane un Sphinx & aux...
...lutarque, ainsi que dans Cicéron , dans Sénèque & même la Tour d'Andronic Cyrrhe-
Delà vint cette prodigieuse...

...niaton rapporte que de tous temps les Phéniciens sacri...quemment sur les monumens...
...élémens ... vents , le culte qu'ils... rendoient fur...ailles Phéniciennes ou Puni-
...celui de Vesta , de la Terre &c. ; qui les Etrusques passa...médailles ont ordinairement...
...des quels les Romains l'emprunterent ; les Vents con...nées aux flancs , & les deux...
...ne des Génies , ainsi que... Dieux que l'on regardois...qui supprimerent les pre...
...eu des hom...habitans de ... du Ciel...

(11) Distr...

Les Isle...
plus d'agrém...
...icres, con...

...suite par ce qu'elles donnoien...

que ceux de...ec des ailes (18) Ces pamp...
qui avoient...des Dianes ailées : Méduse...
qui étoient...avec ces attributs que les G...
les Grecs , à... à l'Amour , & quelquefois...
...tot, dans p...comme on le peut voir sur...
dans Virgile...te encore à Athenes (20) .
Sanchon...
...fioient aux a...s, de même que sur les méd...
l'origine de...es Génies qu'on voit sur ces...
chez les Sal...deux des quelles sont attac...
...sidérés com...paules ; les artistes Etrusqu...
comme des l...

, les Villes & les Endroits...
plu...

...daglie Maltesi.

...Etrusques av...
de Vénus ,
...eprésentées
la Victoire ,
Vents (19)...
tes qui subsi...
quantité de...pour être le terme de tou-
des Etrusque...ation successive de tous les...
...ques (21) I s appelloient la Grande An-
quatre ailes , instruits pouvoient prévoir...
autres aux é...pendant lesquelles il y avoit...

Today You Will Not Die a Horrible Death

CJ Evans

There's only this one guarantee
in the body—this moment. And I grip

the indeterminate thing in my hands
and ask it to last somewhat longer.
And I try not to consider the time itself;

the way it writhes against my cumbersome
holding, but rather you, not your face

that will move into the spreading milk,
but how I'm loved somehow, knowing that,
being sure if only in that. And as I do

this one thing no one could demand
I do differently, I ignore the pull,

even as my moment halves and halves
again, to look ahead. I'll take with me
whatever part of you I've taken already

as I walk into the memory of elephants,
as I go to hide behind their gray legs.

Him Can We Save

The pines are quiet
in the Canyon of Wolves

and the laughing girls
sleep, their faces hidden

by overcast memories
of anis. The volcano

readies, empties
its matchboxes

on the floor and waits
patiently for the drought

to come. The sky
jostles and he drinks

deep from the taste
of gunmetal. He steps

again through the secret
passage; he is looking

for something. It's
never where he looks.

Meherangarh

Zachary Lazar

The Murder Victim

HIS NAME WAS WYATT SUMNERS. WHEN THEY FOUND HIM, HE had just turned fifty—he had seemed younger than that the one time I met him. It was a few months ago, at Vikram and Caroline Aggarwal's house in Jodhpur. The Aggarwals live in an eighteenth-century palace decorated with handmade furniture and textiles, each object specially chosen, resonant with the taste of someone who looks at objects every day as a profession. There must have been forty rooms in the house's new addition, a rectangular court built around the original *haveli* with its intricate screens carved into the sandstone walls.

Sumners sat on a low sofa dressed in jeans, a zippered leather jacket, and a cotton scarf that looked like it came from the local market. In London, he had been an unsuccesful actor, but now he was a tutor, or as he put it, a "babysitter" for the two children of a movie producer I work for—that's what had brought us together that night, a movie I had cowritten, set in India. Vikram Aggarwal and I were talking about politics and Sumners was sipping his wine, admiring the room. I was speaking about things I knew nothing about, haz-arding opinions in the broad way you fall into when you read the paper in foreign countries, even ones you've set a screenplay in. The news that week concerned separatist fighters in the state of Assam. In an act of ethnic cleansing, they had gunned down seventy migrant farm workers from the state of Bihar. The United Liberation Front of Asom. I said if I had not happened to be traveling in India that week I would never have heard of the United Liberation Front of Asom.

Sumners sighed. He had been in the country for three months and was exhausted by it. "All I want is my week on the beach," he said. "Then I'm off to Mallorca with the two brats."

He lit a joint and offered it to me. Unshaven, his hair long enough to be feathery, he had that ironic cheerfulness that people from everywhere have now, like Americans on TV, which like a common language softens the differences between us.

"Where are you going, Goa?" I asked.

"Yes. You've been there?"

"Not for a long time. Maybe twenty years ago. More than that actually. Before it was Goa."

None of the seventy murdered Biharis' names was mentioned in the papers. In ten days, it was Sumners' name that would be mentioned in the papers.

Citadel

The main site to see in Jodhpur is the Meherangarh Fort, which looks like something from a movie. From a distance, it's the beige color of the desert behind it, as are the ancient city walls with their watchtowers. On the ground floor, inside iron gates high enough for elephants to pass through, are rows of women's handprints inscribed on the wall in a rectangular pattern. They're there to commemorate the widows who committed suttee, the ritual of throwing themselves on the pyres of their husbands killed in battle, defending the fortress.

Each ruler built another palace on top of the last. The fort is so tall you take an elevator to the top, and the view from there makes modern skyscrapers seem like the work of barbarians. Along certain ledges you can see the full height of the highest towers, cream-colored, shaped like minarets, and the cubed-shaped buildings of Jodhpur below, all of them painted blue. Someone had to place the carved stones that high up in the air. Someone had to whitewash them each year after the monsoon. The maharaja's wives would lift ornate dumbells to keep themselves slim, or lounge on divans beside marble fountains, their lives spent behind the screened walls of a fortified harem thirty stories high.

Hollywood

For three months—October to December—the actors and crew for the movie I'd helped write had been in Jodhpur, shooting on location at the Bal Samand Palace Hotel. The movie was a sex comedy—there was no special reason it had to be set in India, other than that it would give us an excuse to go there, and without the setting it would be indistinguishable from twenty other movies just like it. Caroline was telling stories about the reaction of the locals, the way everyone knew the names of even the minor stars, the director, the screenwriters—even me, who had not arrived until it was all but over. The merchants had sold the producer and his wife three hundred bed covers. One of the stars, a famous comedian, had bought so much jewelry in one of the shops that the owner had given him the key. He was able to lock it up day and night if he wanted, so no one else could go in.

"How did you settle on Jodhpur?" Wyatt Sumners asked.

"That was Wilentz's idea," I said, passing him back the joint. "I had it set in Khajuraho at first, where they have those temples with the erotic carvings. There were a lot of Kama Sutra jokes we had to cut out."

Sumners took the opportunity to denigrate our boss. "Wilentz must have seen a way to save money," he said. "Probably did a deal with the local council. The mayor."

"It's not the mayor," said Vikram. "The man he would have talked to is called the collector. I always loved that word."

"Sounds like Kafka," said Sumners.

"At least he didn't do a deal with the collector of Assam," I said.

We were still sitting in the large room that opened onto the courtyard. Two great danes lay on their sides on pale green beds trimmed with silk thread. Fires burned in iron bowls, six on either side of the lawn. We had eggplant salad, goat cheese, spring rolls with cilantro and shaved carrots. We drank wine from Caroline's home in Chile. Her five-year-old daughter Lucinda came down and spoke to us in

Hindi. She could count to thirty in three languages. Her favorite food was macaroni and cheese.

Sumners was going to take the train to Goa that week, rather than fly. In one of the many peculiarities of Indian travel, he reminded us, second class A/C was better than first class. It must have been around this time that I told the story of Veronica and me on the train platform in Udaipur.

The Rani of Mandi

Rajasthan is poor, in spite of all the talk you hear about India's boom. On the road to Jaipur, the capital, you can see almost a mile of ruins on either side of the road where audiences used to watch processions enter the city on elephant back. The elephants would have been caparisoned in red and green and their riders would have been swathed in jewels. Legions of weavers and masons and carvers and musicians had been supported by that way of life, before cars and motorcycles joined the bullock carts and stray dogs on the broken roads. Now the palaces are dilapidated, even a major site like Meherangarh Fort is only partly restored. I remember walking through the empty halls, Veronica and I, through the room of baby cradles, the room of palanquins, the room of Belgian mirrors, the room of arms and armor—daggers, lances, swords. In one of the rooms was an exhibit of antique photographs, portraits of the old royal families. One was of a woman called the Rani of Mandi, on the occasion of her appearance before the court of George V in 1924. She was dressed in a pale sari—I imagined it for some reason as gold— extending one hand behind her hip as if to brush back her veil, the other hand at her breast, clasping a pearl necklace. It may have been that her hair was only pulled back, but it was possible to imagine it as cut short, like a flapper's, like Zelda Fitzgerald's.

On the Platform

We were waiting for a train in Udaipur, Veronica and I, when we had one of those moments you never want to have, moments of revelation, disgust. Udaipur itself is a tourist city, "the Venice of India," built on a lake that encircles one of the world's most famous hotels.

Outside the station it had been unusually quiet, almost no one there, but on the platform there was a throng of carts being steered by porters, tea sellers, men with turbans and walking sticks, teenage boys in windbreakers and jeans. It happens all the time in India, the stares of men and boys, an unreadable gaze that is usually nothing more than curiosity. On the streets of a place like Udaipur, it's easy to behave like a child sometimes, smiling and answering when someone asks what country you are from, as if the question is innocent, as if you are glamorous, maybe even a movie star. Your choice in a crowd in India is often to be a child or a hostile intruder.

At first there were maybe fifteen boys, but soon there were more than thirty, moving in closer, like birds, until they had formed a semi-circle around us as we stood with our luggage, everything dim on the platform, just a few lights behind the crowd of faces. They began to make longer and longer eye contact, more emboldened as they saw how little there was we could do. They were staring right at Veronica, her long hair coming down over her shoulders, American hair. I waved my hand and said "goodbye," as if being sarcastic, but they knew sarcasm and weren't moved. A small boy in glasses watched me, enthralled, a nervous smile on his lips, waiting to see how I would react. My glance was enough to shame him into averting his eyes, but only a moment later he was staring again, knowing that he was safe within the mob.

I made eye contact with the leader, a tall, lanky boy with a scarf tied around his head like a bandage. I told him to back off.

"This your wife?" he said.

"Move away."

"How many times you make baby with your wife?"

I don't remember a single woman being on the platform. Everyone was a man or a boy, all of them watching now, even those who were by the newsstand twenty yards away. The boy with the scarf on his head was shaking he was so excited, smirking and pacing, knowing that no matter what I did, everyone was on his side.

The Shrinking Globe

The Rani of Mandi grew up in a town called Kapurthala in a palace designed by a French architect who modeled it after Versailles. She was the child of her father's fifth wife—his fourth wife was a dancer from Spain, his sixth an actress from Prague. The Rani's father, the Maharaja of Kapurthala, spent a quarter of his annual income on jewels. The Rani was his only daughter. She was sent to England for her education, spoke several languages, had friends in Hollywood, New York, all over the world. In 1940 she was living in Paris, then the world's most cosmopolitan city, when the Nazis invaded. Some of her closest friends were Jews, and in an effort to save them the Rani bartered all of her jewels to help them gain passage to the United States. The plan was uncovered by the Gestapo, who deported the Rani to Germany. It had taken just a single moment—the moment of her arrest—to strip away everything I have just told you about her. She was detained in a concentration camp, where she died after only two months.

"Did you read that?" Veronica said, showing me the caption at the exhibit.

I hadn't read it. I had walked right by the photograph, seeing just a beautiful woman in lavish clothes, a kind of Indian Zelda Fitzgerald, I'd thought.

The Mob

They call it "Eve teasing" in India—whistling, groping, fits of sexual aggression toward women. The play of gazes, back and forth, becomes distortive, intensifying, compulsive—everyone involved becomes somebody else. At the time, it seemed that anything could have happened, that when the train came the men and boys could have rushed into our compartment and taken turns with Veronica, and in the face of their stares it was hard to decide if the danger was all just imagined. The only thing to do was to decide that it was.

Convivium

We drank many bottles of wine that night at Vikram and Caroline's. They were an easy group of people to talk to, though we came from different places all over the world. At dinner there was Szechuan chicken, prawns in garlic sauce, a salad with beets and greens grown in Vikram and Caroline's garden. Serge and Alain, two Parisians, dealers in antiques, arrived from the airport. Their white shirts and black pants and mustaches reminded me of the cotton brokers in Degas' paintings. Their clothes were so clean they shone.

"We were four days in the Delhi aiport," Serge told us. "Fog for four days. They would keep us on the runway, then back to the gate, then back to the runway."

I felt wrong about telling the story of the station in Udaipur. It had disturbed everyone, raised the specter of xenophobia, not just the men's and the boy's but mine. Everyone agreed that what had happened was rare, so rare it was almost unheard of. It was better to talk about Indian films, as we were now (everyone had seen the films of Deepa Mehta, banned from Indian theaters). We talked about Bollywood, the rival stars Shahrukh Khan and Amitabh Bachchan, Bachchan's son Abhishek's impending marriage to the superstar Aishwarya Rai. They formed a kind of royalty, these stars. They held stakes in the nation's corporations and could sway the outcome of elections. Like the weather, movie stars were something you could always talk about in India. Even Wyatt Sumners could talk about Aishwarya Rai.

"Stunning," he said.

"The most beautiful woman in the world," said Serge, bored, reaching for the wine.

"Not far from it," Sumners said. He pushed some arugula onto his fork. "You know, they named a tulip after her in Holland."

I thought, if it hadn't been for Sumners, and his trip to Goa, I would not have told the story about the station in Udaipur. I resented him a little for my own lack of tact, knowing I had no justifiable reason for feeling that way. I felt it anyway. When I think about it now, I realize there are no limits to my carelessness, my ignorance. I realize that if I hadn't co-written a screenplay set in India—a sex comedy like twenty others—Sumners would never have been there in the first place. He would presumably still be alive.

OPEN CITY

The Papers

Sumners was found in a small village outside Goa, hung by his neck from a mango tree. According to the papers, a group of men had either trailed or driven him to that place of huts and cook fires—sixty miles from the beach hotel he'd been staying at—and clubbed him to death, then hung him with a sari from the branches. The police beat confessions out of four suspects, whose stories were garbled, contradictory. One account said that Sumners had made a sexual advance on a local woman. Another that Sumners was buying and selling drugs. As motives reported in a newspaper, these are rational enough to help us stop thinking about the crowbar in the teeth, the feet kicking at the side of the still body. Perhaps the only real explanation is the simple one, that some grievance or misunderstanding had erased the basic assumptions that hold true most of the time, almost anywhere: that people are more or less the same, that kindness or reason will bridge their differences. The suspects who gave confessions were almost certainly innocent themselves. What we know for sure was that Sumners had called home to England the night before he died. He said he was on his way to Bombay to see a fireworks show.

Cosmopolis

I forgot to mention that there were guards posted inside the gates of Vikram and Caroline's house when we arrived. I don't know if they were armed or not. My first impression was not of the guards but of the lavish grounds—the stone gate high enough for an elephant to pass through, the endless lawn where fires burned in two rows of iron bowls. It looked idyllic (in a way, it was idyllic, all those strangers from everywhere, so easy to talk to). I forgot to mention also that Vikram was part of the local royalty, a nephew of the current Maharaja of Jodhpur. I remember later that night thinking of the Rani of Mandi, of how I had taken her at first for a kind of socialite, someone you might see nowadays in a newspaper or on TV. I think now that in some way this is what prompted me to tell the story of the train platform in Udaipur. In part of my mind, I was carrying the image of the Rani's face at the court of George V, knowing, as I knew by then, what had become of her, of her friends and their world, knowing how defenseless it had turned out to be. Gathered at Vikram and Caroline's house, we seemed in the light of the Rani's story feckless, childlike. The night was beautiful. Its beauty was protected by a gate, and to be on the right side of that gate involved nothing more than luck. Everyone knows this. Everyone knows that luck doesn't last.

Train

When the train pulled into the Udaipur station, there was a decision to be made as to whether or not we should get on. The first few cars were already so full of people that they were hanging out of the doorway, holding onto the frames, the train still advancing. The pack of boys around us dispersed and moved in a scrum toward the tracks, matching the train's pace, luggage clutched to their chests with one arm, their free arms outstretched. It was like watching a sport, or like watching footage from a war. They leapt up into the crowd that was already on the train, a tangle of bodies spilling out of the opened doors—scarves, bundles, rags.

"Let's go," said Veronica.

"You're sure."

"Yes. Hurry up."

In our berths in second-class A/C, the couchettes were made of clean blue vinyl, with a stack of pillows and sheets and blankets and a towel. It was as quiet as the waiting room of an office. I tried to read. The newspaper was full of ads for high-rises in Bombay, luxury apartments with backup power and three tiers of twenty-four hour security. After awhile, the train bumped forward, then slowly moved on into the darkness with a steady, thudding rhythm that invited sleep. Everything seemed far away. Before long it was possible to forget that ahead of us, separated by just a few doors, was the mob of men and boys, crammed into the compartments with bare feet, squatting in the aisles, twisting and hanging from the rails.

We Traveled by Night in a Ship Made of Ebony Splinters

Dara Wier

We watched an octopus pretending to be sleeping.
It was watching us pretending we weren't noticing.
Our walls were to our windows what our mouths were to our minds.
In the distance ivory glowed across the horizon as if a supernatural light
source were being tested.
You were perhaps the one in charge of this document.
So I cut my finger for you to surprise you.
In the distance tingled acres of red-tipped monolithic bee storms.
I saw you duck behind the tree of a cypress.
I saw you corner and quarter and replace yourself with a turnstile.
Much makes us miss your velocity and endurance.
I have a little pocketful of your steadfast resolution.
In the distance are horses convening, as snow falls off them
and you fall on us and we stand here as though we were taking it.

They Like to Say Light Is Your Shadow

You are now somewhat officially abstracted. In this way
You function somewhat in the manner of several mirrors.
You do to us little more than we do to petrified forests.
We identify, plunder, photograph, analyze, ionize and pocket you.
You shout out for us out of all of our poor blue projections.
When we are unfamiliar with you we attempt to address you
By calling upon names familiar, at the ready, and wrong-twisted
Though we know this is no way to approach you, we do it
And little comes of it. I saw you nine times in black stripes
In blue caves in broken open snowbanks. I called you Big
Monkey Currency Captive Primitive Handshake. Once more
You adorned me with another of your brutal harsh brush-offs.
You ignored me. We consoled me. You returned our compliments.
You slipped yourself systematically back into your prison of fevers.

Something for You Because You Have Been Gone

What happens to us when you go away goes something
Like what happens to shoes in a dead man's closet.
Things inert without breath or breeze to stir them.
As if at the striking of a bell or the blow of a whistle
Or a shot from a pistol everything moving comes to a
Standstill. Quite some race this. Impossible to find
A decent seat. We thought about betting the farm
On who or what might make the first move. We
Were never 100% all there before, why would we want
To be that now? It looks like a struggle ensued where
The hair went down. Ah, look at where so many choose
To leave their skins behind. We passed along a few blankets,
An armful of unworn blouses. We passed you from hand
To hand and solemnly swore to unmention your name.

The Spirit of St. Louis

You're like dust I lift off with my fingers from a black
Frame. You're like lint I find on my knees after kneeling
Beside a table to pick up something I've dropped. Come on,
Grant us one wish. You are the size of a seed, a small one, one
That's been frozen for centuries. A thread cut from the hem
Of a handmade dress, an eyelash, one scale sticking to the cuff
Of a fisherman's shirtsleeve. You are a black grain of sand.
On the cheekbone of a girl sitting in front of a fire. In firelights
of heatwaves and smokescreens and downdrafts come you
Miraging. We hear the steady whir of you as you pass
Overhead descending. You sound as if you're moving with
No end in sight something heavy over rough ground. Stone
Gone somewhere on the outer edges of other outer edges.
Chills bristle and chills break and I write your name in a book.

Mutant Architecture

Audrey Salmon

from **Dear Photographer**

Jason Labbe

(text message)

The lonely go unlisted
while blonde beauties like you perfect
invisibility. Outside the office

I don't carry a phone because
    a) I am afraid it will ring
    b) I am afraid it will not ring

Forget my desk extension.
Is a skyscraper still
the most connected

kind of structure.
Decreasingly
laced in cables, no longer

bathed in continuous waves,
the workday streams in
bits, bytes, pixels.

No filthy satellite or cell tower
can transmit
your new ocean pictures

OPEN CITY

(depth of field)

Departure is the farthest
point in the field,
the hard-to-see

detail on the horizon
that disappears
with overexposure.

Is that one head
lifting out of the grass
or two

Do You Hear What I Hear?

A. M. Homes

SHE HEARS THE CAR BEFORE SHE SEES IT. THE SOUND DRAWS HER
to the window. It's dusk, the headlights are on; two eyes staring down
the long road. When they hit a bump, they vanish momentarily as if
blinking. The twilight sky is a pitch perfect blue that hums. In front
of her house, the late model black sedan slows, then parks. No one
gets out. She peeks from between the Venetian blinds. When she
pushes down the blind to get a better look, the old metal bends with
a loud crack, startling her. The car's headlights are still on, staring
down the street like someone lost in thought—daydreaming.

Maybe they are not who she thinks they are, maybe there are here
for some other reason, maybe it has nothing to do with her. But it's
not everyday a late-model car pulls up outside and just sits there.

She gets binoculars. By the time she's back at the window, the
headlights are off, but now the interior light is on. She spies two men
wearing suits and black hats. The driver is resting his arms on top of
the wheel and the other one is reading a newspaper. She focuses the
binoculars—reading over his shoulder so to speak. Sports. She
watches for a few minutes, nothing happens. She goes back to what
she was doing—what ever that was. She can't remember. Twenty
minutes later when her doorbell rings she's caught off guard with
depilatory cream on her upper lip, defoliant she calls it. She wipes off
the Nair and goes to the door.

"Who is it?" she asks.

"You called," one of the men says.

"I called two days ago," she says.

"We're not full time," the man says.

She opens the door, "Well, I thought it might be you. I saw the car pull up, but then no one got out."

One man gestures toward the other. "He was listening to his radio show."

"You had the interior light on," she says.

"So I could read the paper. I don't like to be left in the dark."

"Come in," she says. The men check left and right before entering. She spots her binoculars on the floor and kicks them under the sofa.

One of the men takes his hat off; he's got another hat on underneath. She wonders if he's Jewish or undergoing chemotherapy. "I've got a head cold," the man says," feeling her stare.

"That can happen just about any time of year," she says. "Are you from around here?"

"Not far," he says.

"Not from here," the other man says. "It's easier for us to do our work if we're not natives, not too familiar, we're less likely to miss a clue if it's all new to us."

"Have a seat."

The two men sit side by side on the edge of the sofa.

"How's the weather been?"

"Off and on," she says. "Not so long ago we had an odd one—there was a rushing sound, folks said it sounded like a twister, except it was bright white, like a snow cloud in an otherwise empty place. It blew through a shield of hail, like a single plate of shattering glass, a lot of sound, hail stones like baseballs, and in five minutes the sky was clear again.

"Atmospheric bloat and purge," the taller, thinner of the two men says.

"And last Thanksgiving we had that freak snow cone that dropped crushed ice everywhere."

They nod. The taller of the two, reaches up over his shoulder and without turning his head, plucks a bug out of the air and squashes it bare handed.

"Would you like a tissue?" she asks.

He takes a handkerchief from his pocket and deposits the dead bug into it, refolds the hanky and puts it in his breast pocket. "I've got it," he says, patting his pocket. "Must have got in when you opened the door."

"How about a cup of tea or a cookie?"

"You wouldn't have a Dr Pepper would you?"

"Yes I do. I've got one hundred percent authentic Dublin Dr Pepper—oldest Dr Pepper plant in the country."

"And the only one still using imperial pure cane sugar—makes a difference."

"Make that dos Dr Pepperos," the other man says. She notices that he's got a foreign accent.

She dips into the kitchen and returns with two tall bottles of Dr Pepper—she pops the tops and hands a bottle to each man. "May I ask your name?"

"Serge," the one with the foreign accent says.

"Katherine," she says, tapping her hand to her chest. "But you already knew that from the call."

The men sip their Dr Peppers in silence.

"Mumm," the other man finally says. "Tom Mumm." He takes another sip and looks around the room. "Is that one of those Radioshack pictures?" he nods toward a painting on the wall.

"How do you mean?" She asks.

"Radioshacks, the psychological test. You look at it and it tells you if you're nuts or not."

"Actually my cat made it—I had a cat who liked to paint. I'm not sure how she picked her colors but they turned out pretty good. She passed a couple years ago, but her work lives on. I could show you a video of her working—they made one for public television."

"It looks like flowers in a vase," Serge says.

"I was going to say spiders leaving the web," Tom says.

A cat comes out, flicks his tail against Mumm's leg. Mumm cries out. "What cat is that?"

"It's the neighbors—they're never home so it hangs out here. Doesn't paint though, just eats and poops. I gave it a litter box with antenna, rabbit ears, it's a little joke between me and the cat." Katherine is the only one who laughs.

"And that?" Serge asks pointing to something hanging off the wall.

"The hand of fate," Katherine says. "I made it myself. I poured hot wax into surgical gloves and let it cool.

"Unusual flowers." Mumm nods to the blue carnations next to the hand of fate.

"I made those too—with food coloring." I like them because they exist nowhere in nature. That's why I like it here—this part of Texas is like no other place in the world.

Serge chortles. "Certainly very different from my Russia."

"How did you come from Russia?" she asks.

"On an airplane."

She's not sure that was the answer she was looking for but lets it go.

Serge touches the fabric on her sofa. "Opulent," he says, practicing his pronunciation.

She smiles. "I go to Europe every year during the month of July— it's too hot here, and everything there is on sale, you can get bits and pieces. I'm a gatherer. I gather things

"And that's how you make a living?" Mumm asks.

"I give piano lessons."

"What's the cat's name?" he asks.

"Dusty short for Dostoyesvsky."

"Is that Polish for something?" Mumm asks, no one answers. "What is this place anyway?" he asks, suddenly crabby, put out, defensive as though he embarrassed himself with the Polish joke. "Where the heck are we?"

"It's a stop on the road to nowhere," she says. They used to call it tank town—a water stop for the railroad. They say the town was named by a railroad engineer's wife who took the name from *The Brothers Karamazov,* others will tell you the town was supposed to be Martha, but the person who named it had a speech impediment and so it came out Marfa, and there is a another faction who point to a character in a book by Jules Verne. Any which way you look at it it's the stuff of fiction," Katherine says. She once again glances out between the blinds. "So is that your car out there?"

"Why not leave the questions to us?" Mumm says.

"Your lights are on."

"Shit." Mumm opens the door, steps outside and claps loudly, dogs bark—the lights turn off.

"He's always up to something," Serge says.

Mumm comes back into the house, closes the door and locks it.

She is suddenly a little nervous. There's a shift in his demeanor.

"We came about the call. We have reason to believe that he's been here before, that he likes Texas."

"How long have you lived here?" Serge asks.

"My whole life. My mother's father was an early adapter. He bought land a hundred years ago. My father was stationed nearby, learned to fly here during the war. My mother too, she was a military pilot—WASP. I was a late baby. My parents were already divorced when I was born; I was created after the fact. Best sex she ever had is what my mother told me. That's why she never got pregnant before, it just wasn't good enough to make a baby."

"That isn't something a mother should tell her child," Mumm says.

"Should—isn't the word to use, it implies an error has occurred. If she hadn't, then I wouldn't, if you know what I mean.

"About the call?" Serge says. "You got the call."

"Yes."

"Where were you when it happened—were you asleep or awake?" Mumm wants to know.

"I was in the kitchen cooking."

"Could we see the kitchen?" Serge asks.

She leads the men into the kitchen.

"That phone there?" Serge asks.

She nods, yes.

"Yellow, wall-mounted, Bell System, mid-1970s model. Heavily kinked extra long cord." Mumm talks, Serge takes notes.

"I like to talk while I cook," she says.

"I haven't seen one of these in a long time—still works?" Mumm asks, suspicious.

"Never fails," she says.

"Is that blood?" Serge points to something on the receiver.

Mumm licks the phone. "Tomato Sauce," he says. And then wipes the phone with a cloth from his pocket.

"My grandmother was Italian," she says.

"Mine too," Serge says.

"Was the room like this before the call or was that something that just happened?" Mumm gestures floor to ceiling, indicating the glossy white macaroni decoupage that covers everything.

"I worked on it for years," she says, pulling open a drawer and showing the two men her glue gun. "While things cooked, I glued and then I painted. It's pretty durable, every now and then it gets a chip and I repair it. Long ago, when I was in kindergarten we made macaroni pencil cups for our grandparents. I still have the one I made for my grandmother—glued macaroni onto a Campbell's soup can and spray painted it gold—Andy Warhol may have been the first one to the bank but he was not the only one who saw gold in them there hills."

"Going back to the call, what time would you say it came in?"

She shrugs. "Sixish."

Serge sprays the phone with something he takes from his pocket.

"Are you dusting for fingerprints?" she asks. "It wasn't a burglary. As far as I know, no crime was been committed."

"We have to investigate," Mumm says.

"Actually, I'm germ phobic and you saw what happened before— he licked it." Serge says.

"Taste buds are smart buds," Mumm says.

"It's Listerine," Serge says, spraying and wiping, spraying and wiping. "I ran out of Purell."

"When you called us where did you call from?" Mumm asks.

"I called from here. I was in a panic, well, not really a panic but in a state. I certainly called from a state."

"Lets go back over it from the beginning," Mumm says. He puts his Dr Pepper down on the kitchen table and opens his briefcase. It's soft sided, more like a large zip-lock bag. She didn't realize he'd been carrying it with him. She hadn't noticed it at all. And yet, it's fixed to his wrist, with a cable tie almost, as though handcuffed there. She can't help but stare, it's awkward as Mumm twists his hand around trying to open the bag. She's not sure if she should offer to help or not.

He catches her eye. "I lose everything," he says. "Been that way since my mitten clips." He finally gets the bag unzipped and takes out a notepad and a heavy red leather bound book, puts the book on his lap, notepad on top, and then withdraws a ballpoint pen from his pocket.

"You don't have to write on your book, you can use the table," she says.

"That's okay," he says, "It's the good book. I carry it everywhere."

"Not only does he carry it—he sells it, in a fine leather binding. We've got a trunk full." Serge says.

"I've got the book as well as some nice hairbrushes if you need one, from my previous position."

"You were a hair stylist?"

"No," Mumm says. "Door to door sales—in the evenings after work. If you need anything later, when we're done, we've got it all in the trunk. Okay, so you don't have caller ID. Did he identify himself."

"Not overtly," she says. "At first I did think he was trying to sell me something—I just couldn't figure what. He never seemed to zero in on a particular product."

"Did he speak of a certain kind of hunger, any mention of desire or confusion and contradiction to what he said?"

"No."

"Did he swear at you or use dirty or abusive language?"

"No."

"Speak about himself as the father of man?" Mum asks.

She shakes her head, no.

"Any mention of a position you should assume?"

She is confused.

"Down on your knees?" Mumm asks.

"Did he seem in any way ironic, amused, mocking?" Serge asks before she answers.

"No."

"Did you enjoy the conversation, did it leave you feeling lifted or other wise transformed?"

"I felt okay at first, a little surprised, caught off guard, and then later it started seeming stranger and stranger."

"About how long of a conversation was it?" Serge asks.

"I really don't know—it was like everything suspended during it."

"Ten minutes or two hours?" Mumm asks.

"Yes."

"Did he mention speaking again in the future?"

"He neither ruled it in or out."

"Do you feel you know or understand him any better and or that he had a deeper understanding of you?"

"Not so much."

"Was there a confessional aspect, did you tell him secrets, things about yourself that no one else knows?"

She shakes her head.

"Any sense of menace or threat?"

"None."

"Did the subject of plagues come up?"

"No plagues."

"Any mention of wrath?" Mumm asks. "Judgment . . . a sense that we were getting it wrong—disappointing him?"

She shakes her head.

"Do you remember anything about the tone of his voice, did he sound annoyed, amused, intrigued?"

"Mild. I would say he sounded mild."

"How were things left, was there a sense he'd call again now that he's got your number—did he mention getting your number from someone, having some kind of connection to you?" Serge asks.

"Did you get the feeling he's done this kind of thing before—or are you the first?"

"Was there any kind of tone at all, beyond omniscient, beyond neutral?"

"I'd have to call it apologetic."

"Did he ask for anything—were there any demands?"

"He wanted nothing."

"Were you frightened by the call—did you feel it told you something, compelled you to a certain behavior? Excuse the pun—but did it feel like a calling—as in, you were called upon, that you were being asked to do something."

"After the conversation did you have the sense that all things are one?"

"Does he have any kind of memory—did he recall or refer to past incidents or visits?"

"Did he refer to himself as a creator?"

"Did the person you spoke with give you a name—or otherwise indicate how he liked— I am assuming it was a he—to be identified?"

"He seemed to think I already knew who he was."

"Did you star 69 him?" Serge asks.

"Pardon?" she says.

"Skip the question; you can't star 69 from a dial, " Mumm says, rebuking Serge.

"You have to know when not to ask a question. You have to learn the meaning of N/A—not applicable. Or irrelevant."

In an effort to interrupt Serge's dressing down, Katherine injects herself into the conversation. "I have a princess phone upstairs in the bedroom. It's a push button."

"But you've used the line," Mumm says.

"Yes."

"Drop it, let sleeping dogs die." Mumm says. "Okay, so just to review. You were in the kitchen when the call came."

"Actually, I think I was in the bathtub. I heard the phone ringing, I got out and walked dripping across the floor."

"I thought you said you had just come in the door?" Serge says.

"I had you in the kitchen cooking macaroni and glue." Mumm says.

She points to hot tub just outside the kitchen window in the yard. "I was soaking in it. Are you finding my story so inadequate that you're making one up for yourself?"

"Bad habit, " Mumm says. "We get ahead of ourselves, fill in the blanks. Okay, so you came in wrapped in a towel, flushed from the bath, the phone was ringing, you answered the phone and dropped the towel, all eyes were on you."

"Hello?" she says, baffled.

"I think you changed your channel and started singing a different tune," Serge says to Mumm.

"Did I? My apologies. They used to say I had an eight-track mind. Tom Mumm, my mama used to say I'll never understand what goes on in that eight-track mind of yours."

"It's okay," she says. "Maybe I don't really know where I was. Maybe I was lost in thought. It's not like when the phone normally rings you stop to think—where was I before you answer it. The call, the oddity of it, was so overwhelming that in truth I forgot everything."

"Are you a person of faith?" Serge wants to know.

"I never dropped the towel," she says. "Ever."

"Do you have a religious affiliation, spiritual practice, or some kind of habit along those lines?"

"I would describe myself as a person of thought—a thinking person, but not a joiner. The last organization I ever belonged to was the Brownies and that didn't last more than a couple of months. I don't like activities that involve more people than a poker game. When I was young, I did think James Dean was a god and I did hope to be an actress. I even performed a bit. I took up tap dancing. I danced in a show." She stops to catch her breath. "I once had a boyfriend who'd been injured by the same car that killed James Dean."

"The little bastard," Mumm says.

"Dollar in the swear box, dollar in my pocket," Serge jumps in. "You promised to watch your language."

"That's what the car was called, The Little Bastard," Mumm repeats.

"How many times are you going to say it?" Serge asks.

"It was a rare silver Porsche Spyder, the car that killed him."

Mumm and the girl are quiet for a moment, heads bowed in grim remembrance.

"So what did you do immediately after?"

"I phoned my mother. I wanted to see if my phone really was working and I wanted to tell someone."

"And did you reach her?" Mumm asks.

"She was out playing mah jong and didn't call back until the next day."

"Did you tell her about the call?"

"Not in so much detail. I mentioned getting a strange call, she thought it was most likely from someone I dated long ago—one of the boys I liked but she didn't. I reminded her that I was the one who got the call, not her."

"Why did you contact us?"

"I thought you might know something, like if it was a prank or if it wasn't. And I thought you would believe me."

"Oh we believe you, our belief is not the question."

She opens the fridge and takes out a bowl of cherries. "Would you like a cherry?"

"Cherries are out of season," Mumm says.

"A friend FedExs them to me from where they are in season."

"I could never tell a lie to a cherry pie. That's how we learn English in Russia."

"There was a kind of simplicity to the whole thing. The only thing that felt 'off' was that he said, 'one plus one equals one.' I didn't want to be the one to correct him. I think he meant that I is one, which is perhaps a different concept than something we're familiar with. He also spoke about the importance of personal cleanliness, and he talked about tolerating contradiction, the idea that something is and is not all at once."

"I guess it's about how you see things," Serge says. "Through whose eyes, in what world, etcetera, etcetera.

"Do you feel you have exclusive access to something? Do you consider yourself a chosen person?" Mumm asks.

"I'm torn between thinking he is something we create to keep ourselves from being very nervous and lonely and something that actually exists." She glances out the window.

"You're a flower," Serge says, out of the blue. Her skin is delicate, her pores large, like swimming pools, like black tar pits. "It must be hard to keep yourself so beautiful," Serge says.

"Two egg whites and ten minutes", she says.

"What?"

"The egg whites tighten the skin and pull the dirt out. I am not what you assume," she says. "And you no doubt are not who I think you are."

"Why don't we begin from there—admitting that we know nothing, and that our assumptions will get us in trouble," Mumm says.

"Are you alone—are you ever alone? "Serge asks.

"I stand before a mirror questioning myself," she says. "I ask, what do people here want? I answer, a connection, confirmation that who they are and what they believe has a place."

"Are you married?"

"Is that part of the investigation?"

"No, I was just wondering."

"Well, I was going to get married, but then I didn't—I broke it off and I was heartbroken—that's when I re-did the upstairs bedroom. You can go look at if you like. I wanted something warm and old-fashioned like the inside of an Easter egg. Everything here is homemade. I like the feel, the weight of the human hand in my every day life." The two men nod, appreciatively. "How much does what you're just wondering affect the questions you ask?"

"That's a question you have to answer for yourself, about our obligations to each other about what we expect and hope for in our contact and communication with each other," Mumm says. "According to the phone company—you had no call that evening," Mumm says. "What kind of equipment did he use? And why would he have used the telephone when he could just speak to you out of thin air and be perfectly audible."

"I think he was being discrete. He said he was somewhere and that he'd been thinking about things. Why don't you tell me a bit about yourselves—how you ended up being the guys who came here, how you were sent to me—who are you and what do you do?"

"The first thing you need to know is we're real—one hundred percent authentic. You can look us up on the Web, Phenomena Police. We're active-duty officers who investigate calls involving paranormal activity and other phenomena."

"Are you a police officer?"She asks Serge.

"In Russia we have our own techniques, which vary according to the situation. Here I am trying to pass the regular test. There I'm doing different kind of work."

"Like what?"

He makes a gun with his fingers and pulls the trigger. "Bang, bang. Here I have no arms." He shrugs.

Mumm is sweating. Perspiration is suddenly beading on his forehead.

"Must be hot," she says.

"Depends."

"Where do you get a suit like that?"

"Mail order. It's custom, a single suit you wear year round—got places to put ice packs in and a zip-in fleece liner. And it's water resistant, not waterproof, but resistant." He opens the jacket and shows her the inside which is lined with pockets. "Comes with the ice packs. They say you can wear it anywhere from funerals to football games." He plucks a stick of Doublemint gum out of one of the interior pockets. "On occasion, I've been known to use the pockets for other things." Mumm looks up at her. "You've sure got a nice rack on you."

She gives him a sharp slap across the cheek.

"Thanks. Look, I think we've gotten off to a poor start—may I ask for your phone number and would it be all right if I called you sometime?"

"You already have my number and you can call, but if I don't pick up leave a message, and NO hang ups."

He nods.

"Would you like to go to a movie on Friday?"

"My mother is coming to visit"

"I wouldn't mind taking her too, if that's what it takes. Do you like to go see the lights?"

"What lights, like go watch the traffic lights change?" Serge asks. "What about me, you kind of jumped in there, but I was thinking the same thing. I was thinking I'd like to ask you out."

"First come, first served," Mumm says. "Finders keepers, losers weepers. Did they teach you that in ruskie spy school?"

"Are we done here?" she asks.

"I think we're wrapping things up," Mumm says. "We're in touch, so you be in touch."

"Where do you go from here?" she asks.

"To get a bite of dinner," Serge says. "And during dinner we go over our notes, we begin to draft our report. Would you like to come with us."

She blushes. "Thank you, that would be lovely," she says. "Just let me get my coat."

As they're leaving the phone rings, they all stop in their tracks. "What should I do?"

"Let the machine get it," Mumm says.

"I can't," she says. "I was lying. I don't have a machine." She hurries into the kitchen and picks up the phone in the middle of the third ring.

The two men stand in the living room, hats on, ready to go.

"Hello," she says. "How are you? It's good to hear your voice again."

Karen Green

DAMAGING ENACTMENTS

He showed me his birthmark. Quite possibly, it was better than sex. (To his credit, and as a nod to his professionalism, it was unseasonably warm that day, even for the OC. Hence, no camelhair jacket & the unlinked Nordstrom cuffs.) I was nonchalant about it, for a while. No need to rush, we had an hour. I was very nearly suave. We talked about Lots of Stuff, including, yes, my sarcastic "Oh Leslie" utterance, made following solitary-sex-as-self-soothing. His name is Leslie. It's girly in a good way. He wouldn't admit the Oh Leslie Joke was Super Duper Funny, but he did say I was the first patient who had ever told him such a tale. I said, "Excellent". I might've said, "Cool", as well. These are the adjectives I use in therapy. I am middle-aged.

I remarked upon his alluring rolled up sleeves. In the meeting previous, he was wearing cufflinks in the shape of knots, so I never thought I'd get anywhere with him, birthmark-wise. Imagine my delight when he pulled up his sleeve a bit higher for me. It was as good as a Victoria's Secret model tugging at her satin nightie to offer up a glimpse of thigh. I promised not to touch or lick. He said it was weird the way I was committing it to memory, that he was perhaps collaborating w/something he didn't want to be a part of. Excellent. Strangely, at least for me, we were both rather demure during this exchange. I told him I imagined it more Illinois-shaped. He said I was looking at it like I was drawing it. I told him I already drew it, buddy, and it sold. He declined to be photographed. I thanked him, courteously, for the unveiling. I felt reverent, baptized, holy, absurd.

It was smaller and tidier than in my memory. A nice, milk-to-dark chocolate (but not bittersweet) brown, no oxblood tones, not elevated or uneven in terrain, and just a wee bit hairier than the rest of his arm, the hair ever so slightly coarser and darker. The thing is, there were other hairs around it to keep it company, so it didn't look like, say, a McMansion plopped in the middle of a quaint Scottish village. It looked perfectly robust, non-cancerous, and was barely the size of a nickel. (My imagination had it snaking up his arm like some chaotic Fauvist tattoo.) It was NOT shaped like any particular state or country, nor was it scary or menacing in any way. It looked like it could, in fact, have healing properties. It was a friendly island, where someone who had been "shrunk" to the size of a flea could await rescue.

I told him I knew nothing about Quaker miracle meetings before I had that perverted dream about him on Christmas Eve. He said Jung would be proud. I said, "Hey! You were a Quaker, you probably went to one of those meetings, like, when you were a little boy!" He did not confirm or deny. He WOULD not confirm or deny. I made the mistake of telling him I ordered George Fox's BOOK OF MIRACLES (c.1650) online. A pale eyebrow was raised. He wrote something on his pad. *Delusional?* Or, *Tongue-in-cheek Stalker?* I can only speculate. He wrote yet another something after I asked whether he thought my issue was grief, transference or menopause. I did not want him to write the word *MENOPAUSE* in my ever-burgeoning file. I back-pedaled, assuring him that what look like hot flashes only occur in his messy little office, so far.

2

He was Very Mature re: my masturbation story. How delicately, elegantly he parried the ball back to my mucked-up court. With a facial expression as bland as oatmeal, as sand, as a pancake, he Reassured me. He said that just because I'd whacked off (I'm paraphrasing), sarcastically moaned, "Oh Leslie" or "Oh, Leslie", then laughed fiendishly at my own joke all the way through my nightly ablutions, my pill (legal, prescribed) popping, the turning off of lights, (in fact I laughed so hysterically the dogs got really concerned) he told me it didn't NECESSARILY mean I was/am getting WORSE, it's just that I finally did, uh, something to relieve myself On My Own and Told My Own Joke about it to boot. Is this what crones do? I worried for a second he found the whole deal repulsive, but oh well, I had a cheerful Christian Lacroix blouse on, I still fit into small jeans, I wasn't exactly chewing cud or showing him my private parts, I mean other than my psychological privates, plus he makes five bucks a minute.

. . . .

Sidebar:

I'm really learning new things. I'm starting to understand why some people who will remain unnamed get so deeply involved with their own "selves", w/the banal workings of their own partially functioning solipsistic (sp?) brains, why therapy and thinking about therapy and talking about therapy is so freakishly seductive. I've always found other people's problems so much more engaging. But no more! Now maybe I can be a Writer (actually, pretty tedious), a Movie Star, or someone who willingly goes on Dr. Phil to discuss topics like Closure, Empowerment, and Authenticity.

Anyway, back to my session. I like the word, "session", it just sounds healthy. So, I described to him how my brain has been "processing" The Crisis in blacks and whites. To clarify: the choice between, for example, suicide (here are some words you can spell out of the word suicide: die, dies, iced, I.C.U., use, used, dice, dues, Us, I...) and life seems oddly simple nowadays. I used to be able to see the gray in a situation, probably too much gray, considering I just spent a few minutes trying to decide which gray/grey I prefer on the page. But now it just comes down to Fuck or Die. Occasionally, it comes down to Fuck or Die, bitch. But do I want to fuck a stranger? Ew, I do not. Do I want to fuck a dead man? Nope. A Regular Guy? Negative. Someone to whom I write checks to Understand My Unbearable Guilt? Someone who is also Guilty of Imperfect Job Performance (not to be mean, but taking into account the outcome of his previous patient, the one who paved the golden road which led me right into the good doctor's arms I mean office)? Yes! I mean, maybe!

....

Predictably, when he repeated the admittedly crass ultimatum Fuck or Die back to be, in his own dear gravelly voice, I really enjoyed it. It was both excellent and cool. And it brought to mind something from my past, something I had in daily doses, like my special probiotic pills from the health food store, something precious, and, in the end, unenduring. I know what it is/was, it is/was Intimacy. I was just trying to find a word less traveled for it. Intimacy, the word and deed.

....

I believe my well-paid "friend" understands this lack in me very well indeed. Bless him, his birthmark, his invisible conjoined Quaker twin. Bless his lumpy mauve office chairs and his bi-polar info pamphlets scattered on the linoleum, bless his peculiar brown slip-ons, his No Trespassing cufflinks, bless his patience and his schizophrenic patients, bless whatever deviant cards he holds so competently close to his (hairy?) chest. Bless his wife and cute kids. Bless his ECT machines and the science of them, and the magic of them, bless his capacity to heal and fail, bless the laying on of hands, bless convulsions and plastic thingies and mouth guards, the pauses and beeps, the possible results. Bless the possibility of the Unlivable lifting from countless desperate heads, lifting cloudlike or fog-like, or like hair in a Tesla experiment, bless the human fright wig of healing. Sometimes it really works.

·············

Sometimes it works as well as rubbing a balloon on your head and sticking said balloon to the wall.

·············

I have always been fatherless, and, in theory, motherless, but don't tell my mother I said that. On the bright side, if her feelings got hurt, she would make believe it never happened. Still, why untangle those particular Christmas lights? I'm tired.

Once upon a time, I had someone there, who, when my feet got cold, would jump up energetically and retrieve his thickest, most beloved socks. Engrossed, he would roll them on to my waiting, wiggling toes. Afterward, he would pat my feet gently, or put them in his lap and rub them vigorously. During this routine, he would consider my bare toes solemnly, and say, every time, "We have very different nail beds."

....

Once upon a time I had someone who would make a sheet billow for me. Billow is another word I like, its sound and meaning, the muffled tissue paper-ish noise of the cotton, the air disturbing and settling, disturbing and settling, the sheet landing like a parachute on my waiting form. Do it again.

....

Once upon a time I had someone to invent rituals with. We were in the desert, and it was f*ing hot, even at night, and we had a pool. We would take turns holding one another like widdle babies, and walk in slow motion through the warm, shallow water. We had a name for this ceremony: Abandonment Therapy. Sometimes, as I carried him, he would pretend to be afflicted with a degenerative disease and he'd contort his narrow fingers, screw up his face, make cruel noises. There were stars, and bats, and burnished dragon flies, and we didn't think about our future; it seemed endless, or beside the point, or plausible. Our laughter floated along with us, weightless and easy. Sometimes we were naked.

Once upon a time, I had someone who would take off his Disney print underwear, leave on his demolished t-shirt, scoot shyly (after all those years?) into bed and say, "I need a kiss." He'd move toward me in the dark, over the big, stinky dogs hogging the middle, and the male dog would growl possessively. We would laugh toothpaste breath into each other's mouths, and then he'd kiss me and say, "Please don't get sick and die." My response would depend on my mood. Usually, I was in a pretty decent mood. This was before the sleeping pills. I guess it was a long time ago. Once upon a time...oh forget it.

....

My psychiatrist says I should try to dissect why I want to Act Out, do something Bad, something I like to call Naughty, like seduce an inappropriate authority figure or jump

in front of a big (or little, just heavy!) truck. He thinks I should figure out why I don't want to do something good for myself, good AND distracting, like fencing, or swimming with dolphins. Contradictorily, he also pointed out that my being nice/good hasn't got me anywhere, or rather, it got me here. So I say, no more Mrs. Nice Guy, I'm gonna be evil. I'm strongly encouraged to ask myself why it is I desire naughtiness, and why I want that naughtiness to hurt.

....

It just got dark; I hate twilight passionately, never mind the sweet sunset on the mountain, never mind my ghoulish reflection in the window, or the dogs barking at effluvium. Let me take my anti-depressant now and think about it. I have all night.

Why do I want it to hurt? Why am I both too old and too young for this? Why am I so concerned with dignity and grace? What do dignity and grace have to do with fucking and dying? Why am I all talk and no action? Why is art at all important? Why is it so quiet? What can I make with my hands? Where's my wedding band? Why are my hands shaking? Did I forget to turn on the bedroom light? Did I spackle the nail holes? Did I pull the sailcloth curtains closed to keep the night from getting on me? Did I already dream this would happen? Will my insurance cover a simple white room? Why do I want it to hurt? Why do I want it to hurt?

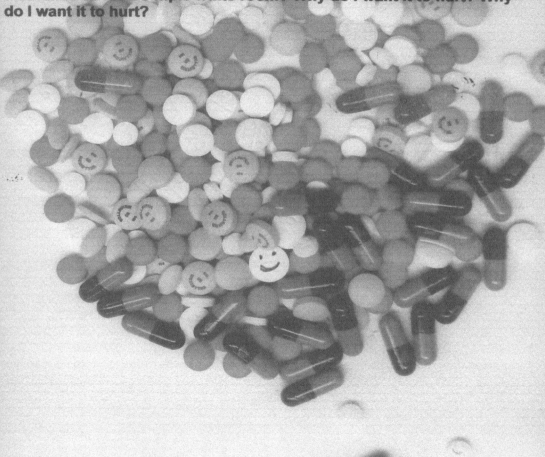

There's a Road to Everywhere Except Where You Came From

Bryan Charles

I ARRIVED IN NEW YORK AFTER A TWENTY-FIVE-HOUR TRAIN RIDE carrying two bags of clothes and a banker's box full of papers. Erin met me at Penn Station and led me through the crush of people and out to the street. We got in a cab and headed uptown. The cab cut through traffic going what felt like eighty miles an hour. Blocks blurred by. Neighborhoods changed. She lived then in a sublet on the upper west side and we pulled off on a pretty street lined with trees and old brownstones. Inside I called my parents and told them I'd arrived safely. I cleaned myself up a bit and Erin took me to get dinner. Back at the apartment we watched TV. I'd barely slept on the train and faded quickly. We got into bed. For a moment I was on one side and she was on the other. Then we slid over into each other's arms. She ran a hand up my back and gripped the back of my neck.

—We're gonna kiss now, she said.

The next day we met Craig at a diner in midtown for lunch. He and Erin caught up a bit. They talked about city life. We finished eating and walked to Craig's office, a minimalist space with bare concrete walls and desks out in the open on a bare concrete floor with a few offices to the side. Everyone wore street clothes and worked on Macs and sat low in their seats staring blankly at big monitors, clicking around at boxes and shapes on the screen. Craig started writing out directions to the place, explaining in detail as he went along. I got confused and was scared to take the subway alone so it was decided I'd come back after he got out of work and we'd go into Brooklyn together. I returned that evening around six and stood on a corner in Times Square loaded down with my bags and clutching the banker's box. Hundreds of people streamed past me and their faces all blurred and I started to feel dizzy and then Craig appeared. He grabbed one of my bags. We went into the subway.

It was a railroad apartment in Greenpoint consisting of a large kitchen, a living room and two open back rooms with no wall or even a sheet between them. The floors of the living room and middle room were covered with worn brown carpet and the floor in the back room was covered with old salmon-colored carpet. There was a pink sponged paint pattern on a jutting section of the wall. In the living room was a futon couch and a small blue chair and a large closet inside of which a TV sat on two Huber Bock beer boxes with clothes hanging all around it. Paul had rigged an antenna and pinned it up with one of his old Kmart nametags. On the wall was an inflatable bull's-eye with Velcro strips and three or four balls stuck to the Velcro. On the floor under the bull's-eye was a plastic cactus in a plastic pot with fake scrub brush. The kitchen walls were half wood paneled and over the sink were copper-colored tiles with images of mushrooms stamped on them. Paul had made a counter from a piece of wood and a large cardboard box. He'd glued the wood to the top of the box and covered the whole thing with an old blue sheet. On the counter next to a coffee maker was a magazine photo of a croissant and steaming coffee and fruit and juice. The photo had been placed in a gold plastic frame. Craig slept in the middle room on a twin mattress on the floor. Also in the room were his stereo and some records and his desk and computer. Ten feet away on the floor under one of two windows was a full-size mattress. It belonged to Paul but he was away till November working a temp-labor gig at a nuclear power plant and so it was temporarily mine. I fell asleep fully clothed that first night under an open window listening to cars hiss by on the street three floors below.

•

Rent was nine hundred dollars split three ways. I cut Craig a check for October's rent which left me with about twelve hundred bucks. I figured this would carry me a while. I decided to get to know the city rather than look for a job right away. Every day I took the train to Manhattan and walked for hours. Often I'd stop and see Erin at work. She worked at a comedy club in the west twenties and sat at a desk in the basement, reading newspapers and smoking and answering the phone. The club was on its last legs and the phone didn't ring much and we'd sit sometimes for an hour shooting the breeze. I'd tell her what I'd seen and done and she'd recommend things to add to my list. I went to Harlem and Times Square and Central Park. I went to a taping of the Ricki Lake Show. I went to the top of the Empire State building and looked out at the city. It was a clear day and I could see to the end of the island. This may have been the first time I saw the World Trade Center in person. I went down there a few days later and stood on the plaza between the two towers and tilted my head and looked straight up. A feeling of vertigo came over me and I almost fell down. A similar sensation began to afflict me on my city walks generally, an odd dislocation, as if my head were a balloon floating twenty feet in the air, connected to my body by a thin string. This balloon head had camera eyes that would record the action and play it back to me. I seemed not to be experiencing events firsthand. This feeling could last an hour or more. I told Paul about it one night over the phone. He said he knew the feeling I meant and described a few times it had happened to him. We gave it a name: the Condition.

Erin took me to a comedy show at the Roseland Ballroom. One of the people on the bill was her ex-boyfriend Stephen. I'd heard a lot about Stephen over the last couple years. She'd moved to New York with him in the late summer of '96, just a few months after she and I split up. She'd always said she thought Stephen and I would get along and I didn't doubt her exactly but I felt threatened by him, by their history together and now his success. We watched his set and had a beer with him later and it was clear within seconds I couldn't hate him, he truly was a good guy. We talked about Kalamazoo and some of our mutual friends. We talked about the Yankess and Chuck Knoblauch's bone-headed move in the ALCS a couple weeks ago, arguing with the umpire while the ball was still in play as Indians' base runners advanced and a run scored. Stephen had been at the game. After the show we stood on Fifty-second Street saying goodbye and I got an odd feeling as we walked away from him, I almost felt sort of sad. On the subway I turned to her.

—Do you think Stephen still likes you?

—Me? She almost laughed. —No I'm pretty sure he's moved on.

A few weeks later I began looking for jobs. My resumé was weak. I had no real work experience and only two publication credits, two poems and an essay, both in obscure quarterlies. And I even fudged it a little—the essay was forthcoming. Nevertheless I applied for every writing and editorial job in the want ads of the three major papers. I received no calls in response. Some jobs I applied for week after week, some every day. There was one job—editorial assistant at Guitar World magazine—that I must have applied for a dozen times. No one wanted me. My bankroll dwindled.

My uncle Art's wife—he'd married a much younger woman, close to my age. I could never bring myself to call her my aunt—had a child-hood friend here who worked in publishing. Her name was Elizabeth and she was an editor at a small children's imprint. Deb put me in touch with her. A lunch was arranged. I met Elizabeth at her office on Astor Place and we walked to a diner called Around the Clock. She was tall and blonde. She was stylish and put-together, and lacked the extra fifteen or so pounds of even the foxiest Michigan babes. As we ate we talked about being new to the city, what the publishing scene was like, what I could do to break in.

—Your mom seems really sweet, she said.

—My mom?

—Yeah. She e-mailed me.

—What?

—Yeah. I assume she got my e-mail from Deb.

—Uh-huh. And what'd she . . . what did she want?

—Oh she just said anything I could do to help you would really be great and if I had any questions or any thoughts I could get in touch with her.

—Questions or thoughts?

—Yeah.

—I see. Well. I guess as long as she's not calling you.

Elizabeth smiled.

—What?

—She called me too.

—Is that . . . did she. And that was what, the same sorta stuff?

—Yeah. Please help my son. I guess she thought I was in a position to hire you or something? I don't know.

I smiled. —Me either.

—You're not mad are you?

—Mad? No. That's not quite the word.

—Good because she told me not to tell you. I just figured . . .

She looked at me. —Aw it's not that bad. She's just worried is all. She's looking out for you. It's sweet.

—It's something.

—Mom why do you do this?

—What?

—You called that girl, Deb's friend Elizabeth? You sent her e-mails?

—I may have sent her one e-mail. Why?

—Why? Are you crazy? Put yourself in my position then ask yourself why.

—Gee I don't know if I appreciate this hostility—

—You know what I don't appreciate? You always calling around behind my back, meddling in my affairs, trying to arrange things for me.

—I don't always call around—

—How do you think it feels to be talking to someone in New York—a publishing person—and suddenly they're telling me my mom's calling her saying—

—Bryan—

—saying please help my son get a job.

—Bryan I think you need to get a grip here—

—Get a grip? Mom—

—I was just trying to help and you act like it's some terrible thing.

—No. It's not terrible. The Nazis were terrible. This is just, I don't even know what this is.

—So now you're comparing me to the Nazis.

—No you're missing the point.

She asked if I at least had a good lunch with Elizabeth, if she had any advice or had given me the names any good contacts. I said stop, you're not listening to me, why won't you listen. She said I am listening and asked what was my point. I told her again and again but knew she wouldn't relent and she didn't. We talked in circles a while longer and then we hung up.

The following week there was a message from Elizabeth asking if I wanted to go to lunch again. I didn't call back. She called one other time and I didn't return that call either and that was the last I ever heard from her.

One day my dad called. He said he was coming up soon. He was dating a woman in New York. Her name was Marsha. She lived on the upper west side.

—It'd be great to see you, he said.

—Yeah.

—I know Marsha'd really like to meet you. I've been telling her about you.

—Is that right?

—Yup yup. But don't worry. Only the good things.

—Ha. Well that's . . . yeah that sounds good.

—How about next Sunday?

—Sunday . . . Sunday. No I don't think I have any plans.

He said he'd talk to Marsha and call me back with the details. He said he was really looking forward to it. I lied and said I was too.

It was decided I'd meet them at Marsha's apartment for breakfast. Sunday arrived, bright and windy and cold. I went into the city and found Marsha's building and stood in the vestibule. I took a deep breath, pressed the buzzer and went in. I heard my dad before I saw him.

—Helloooo.

I climbed the stairs. He greeted me in the hallway and we hugged. He patted me hard on the back. I patted him too. He was grinning.

—This is Marsha.

She stood in the doorway. She was tallish and thin with incredibly curly shoulder-length black hair. Her apartment was small. There was a table with three chairs and places set. Beyond that was a tiny living room, to the left a tiny kitchen.

—Do you want anything? she asked. —Some coffee or we have juice?

—I'll have some coffee.

She went into the kitchen. My dad was still grinning, checking me out.

—Look at you. Mr. Big City Guy.

He chuckled, snorted, shook his head. Marsha returned with the coffee. I stirred in some milk. She and my dad stood there grinning. They both checked me out. Marsha asked about my big move from Michigan. I rehashed a few new to the city impressions. She smiled along like Oh that's so true.

—Anyway, she said. —I'll get started on breakfast. Everything's ready, I just have to make the pancakes. You two sit and catch up. I'll be in the kitchen. It should just take a minute.

My dad sat on the little couch. I sat across from him in a chair. Marsha moved around in the kitchen. I heard batter sizzling. My dad and I eased into empty chitchat. We kept it rolling, old pros by now. He chuckled and grinned and shook his head. Marsha reappeared holding a plate of pancakes. She set them on the table and smiled.

—All right, let's eat.

After breakfast we sat in the living room. My dad put his arm around Marsha. They snuggled on the loveseat and talked about how they met—on the Internet, in a chat room for Jewish singles. Marsha said she had their whole relationship documented. She'd saved all their e-mails from when they were courting.

—Do you ever go into any chat rooms? she asked.

—No.

—No? You've never been?

—No.

—Well. I don't know what your situation is but it's a great way to meet people.

Ten more minutes, I thought. Ten more minutes and I'm gone. We exchanged further bullshit. Chitchat lagged. A weird silence fell, broken by Marsha.

—Shoot, she said. —I almost forgot. I have to run to Duane Reade, I'm, I have to get this prescription filled.

She rose quickly and put her coat on and grabbed her purse from the table by the front door. —You guys'll be okay here, right?

—Sure, said my dad.

—Yeah stay and talk. I'm sure you have a lot to talk about so . . . yeah. Who knows how long I'll be, you never know with Duane Reade, they're often, they can be very slow so. She smiled. —I'll be back.

Suddenly my dad and I were alone. Big alarm bells rang. I felt a sharp pain in my gut and went into the tiny bathroom and sat on the toilet but nothing came out. I took deep breaths and splashed water on my face. Back in the living room my dad was still there. He looked at me and smiled.

—What's up? I said.

—No it's just, it's good to see you.

—Good to see you too.

—We oughtta do this more often.

—Yeah.

—But let's not just say it. Let's make it happen this time. Let's really see each other more often.

—All right.

—We really will. We won't let so much time pass.

—All right.

—So what do you think of Marsha?

—What do I think of her? She's . . . yeah. She seems nice.

—Good. Because we're getting married.

We looked at each other.

—Congratulations, I said.

—Thanks, thank you.

He smiled and sat there. His smile faded somewhat.

—Well there's . . . there's something else too.

I knew what it was but waited for him to say it.

—We're having a baby.

I looked at my dad. He was fifty-four, maybe fifty-five years old. All our interactions had been like this. They'd never been any other way.

—Wow, I said. —Interesting.

The door opened and Marsha came in carrying a Duane Reade bag. She hung up her coat, sat on the couch and smiled. She looked at my father and then looked at me.

—So?

I grinned. I feigned happiness. You could see relief on their faces. Then the mood shifted. She waxed contemplative. She revealed her age—forty-five—and admitted straight-up this wasn't a planned deal. Birth defects were a worry. She was moving to D.C. next month, it was crazy, she never thought she'd leave New York. She knew it was sudden, she knew it must be a shock but I was going to be a big brother and she hoped they'd see more of me, I was part of the family. My dad chimed in. He cosigned the family shit. We sat there gabbing and fake laughing into the midafternoon. They said Let's grab an early dinner, there's a good Indian place. I tapped unknown reservoirs of strength and said sure. We all got up. Marsha went to the bathroom. My dad came over. He stood very close to me. He put a hand on my shoulder.

—I'm know I'm coming at you with a lot here. But I want you to know you're still my son. You're still my number-one guy.

•

After dinner we stood on the sidewalk and my dad suggested we get ice cream. I said it was a long ride to Brooklyn and I should probably get back. Marsha said it was great to meet me and gave me a hug.

—We'd love to see you again soon.

My dad stepped up. He flashed the old grin and hugged me with back slaps.

—All right. Love you.

—Love you too, I said.

I walked two blocks east into Central Park and sat on a bench in the cold. My chest and eyes burned. I rubbed my face. I got up from the bench and walked to Erin's and pressed the buzzer. No answer. I pressed it again. No answer. I hung around on the stoop and looked up at her window. The window was dark. I knew she wasn't home. I lingered another few minutes then walked to the train.

Paul rolled back to New York in November. He brought another mattress, a thin foam thing from a castoff sofa bed. It was only marginally more comfortable than sleeping on the bare floor so he and I switched off, every other night one of us got the good mattress. We placed a single tier of an old brown plastic bookshelf between the two mattresses and loaded it with books and knickknacks. In theory we did this to achieve a modicum of privacy but it was more a dark comment on our lack of privacy than anything else. Occasionally I'd wake before Paul and look over and stare at him and maybe move around slightly waiting for him to open his eyes and see me there staring and when he finally did we'd always crack up. He was flush with dough from his power-plant gig and since technically he'd been laid off he applied for and was granted unemployment. He was in no hurry to find work again and with my job hunt at a dead end we spent many days goofing off in the city. We'd hit the east village record stores two or three times a week. We'd eat cheap lunches at Dojo and the Indian restaurants on First Avenue. I'd go to the Strand and leave with at least one paperback every time. I've always needed a lot of books around and mine were all still in boxes in Michigan. A few weeks of this and my already meager finances were shot. Paul comforted me with tales of his own poverty in the city, which had reached a low point last summer, just before he landed the power-plant job.

—I was living on salads. I tried making pad Thai with a packet of Ramen noodles, crushed peanuts, and soy sauce.

—How was that?

—Horrible. Trish came out in August, I think just to make sure I ate at least a few decent meals.

Paul's grandmother was on government assistance and she sent him a couple big boxes of rations. In our cupboard was a large can with a white label and a silhouette of a chicken. Whole Chicken, it said. There was also a box of government issue powdered milk. Paul had eaten the cheese before leaving for Jersey.

I hadn't written since Michigan and was starting to feel useless so one day when Craig was at work and Paul was out I pulled the large floor speaker Craig used as a chair up to his desk and using his computer wrote for two or three hours. I finished a five-page story about an encounter I'd had many years ago on a hot summer day with a weird girl with scars on her arms who was reading Naked Lunch and told me it was her bible. I called the story Scars, put it through a few rounds of revisions, made copies at Kinko's, checked my list of addresses, and started sending it out to the little magazines.

—And you're able to keep body and soul together?

—Oh yeah. I'm fine.

—Because I can write a check for a few hundred bucks and drop it in the mail first thing tomorrow.

—No no. That's not necessary. I'm good.

—You sure? asked my mom.

—Yeah. I've got a bunch of resumés out. Something's bound to come up.

—All right. Well. Like I say, we're here if you need us.

I'm fine. I'm good. It wasn't true. I was sinking. Faxing resumés daily was a hot ticket to nowhere. December was coming up. Rent and bills would be due. I made an appointment at a temp agency and spent a morning doing their battery of tests. They asked what I was looking for. Anything, I said.

Erin and I rented Austin Powers and Chris Rock's Bring the Pain and watched them at her place lounging in bed and afterward with the lights out we kissed and we took off our clothes. Neither of us had planned on this happening or that's what we told each other anyway but now that it had we couldn't seem to stop. Every time we'd pause and say This should really be the last time. But there was never a last time and it wasn't like before, it was better, we were a few years older and there was an ease to it now. Still the implications scared me. How far could we take this? What did she want from me? What did I want from her? I ignored these questions and brushed aside my doubts and put my hands everywhere and buried my face in her neck and the past was alive in the shape of her body and the dead gods spoke to me through her tongue and her mouth.

I got a temp job with long-term potential. I worked at a law firm at 120 Broadway entering lawyers' timesheets into a database. The pay was twelve bucks an hour. I worked with four women in a tiny office called the Information Center. I sat at a computer and keyed in numbers all day, moving only three fingers of my right hand. On my lunch hour I'd snarf peanut butter and jelly sandwiches from home then wander the tangled grid of streets east of Broadway. If I was feeling rich I'd spring for greasy Chinese food at a little place with seating upstairs in an alley off Liberty Street. Most of the time I'd end up at the Strand's Fulton Street Annex or at a place on Nassau Street called SoHo Books that sold overstock and remainders. Sometimes I'd walk to the World Trade Center and read magazines at Borders and walk around the mall. Being in the mall comforted me. It was like being at the Crossroads Mall in Portage, Michigan, it had a lot of the same stores and all the same smells, new clothes, pungent perfumes and lotions, fast food. The weather was weirdly warm that December and a couple times I got a coffee and sat on the plaza and watched people and looked up at the towers. There was a holiday display set up between the two buildings, three huge words. PEACE ON EARTH.

A couple weeks after I started the other temp quit to pursue acting more seriously. She was replaced the following Monday by a guy named John.

—What'd you do before this? I asked.

—I taught fiction writing.

—Really. Where?

—Arizona State. I was an adjunct. I got my MFA there.

—So you moved here recently?

—A few months ago, yeah.

We started to talk about writing and books. It turned out we liked a lot of the same people. Denis Johnson, Raymond Carver, Tobias Wolff. Then someone came in with more timesheets and we divided them up and got back to work.

I'd had deadening jobs in the past. I worked a summer in the press room at Checker Motors where I stood pressing a button all day punching out car parts. I worked two summers at Georgia-Pacific. I was swing shift there working sixth hand mostly, which meant being present to help clean and rethread the machine when it went down but when it was running well meant long hours of nothing to do or hours of doing busy work like emptying broke boxes or wandering the basement spraying down floors or cleaning out rooms that hadn't been cleaned much less entered in years or simply finding a far off spot to hole up in and wait for the day or the night to pass. Briefly I worked as a sitter at a hospital which meant just that—sitting in a room with a sick or injured person if they requested it, if they or their family wanted them to have company. I sat in a room with a wide-eyed man in a full-body cast and a halo drilled in his skull. He'd been in a car wreck and his mother was there and together we watched a show on cable about the end of days. The screen showed a series of horrific things but the man and his mother agreed the reality would be far worse than anything we could imagine when the Lord finally came. I sat with a blind amputee who was in a kind of coma, sat horrified and staring at the man's leg stumps and was helpless to stop him when he shoved his hand down his throat and began gagging himself. I'd been told how to stop him if this happened but was too scared and yelled out and the nurses ran in. Long before any of that I washed dishes at restaurants and scrubbed toilets at a golf course. The Information Center was worse than all of these things.

—Hey Gina.
  —Yeah Bryan, what's up?
  —I was wondering what the deal was for Christmas.
  —In terms of . . .
  —Well my friend is driving back to Michigan, where I'm from, and I was thinking it'd be good to go with him, maybe take that week off.
  —The week of Christmas?
  —Right.
  —Hmm. That's a bad week, that's our busy time. We're gonna have a bunch of people rushing to get timesheets in before the end of the year.
  —So that's . . . I mean . . .
  —You think there's any way you could stick around?
  —I don't know. I mean I hadn't planned on it.
  —Because, you know, you're doing good here and most likely they're gonna create a permanent data position in the IC and proba- bly you'd be first on the list. Honestly? You take that week off, I have to get someone else to fill in . . . who knows.

Erin stayed too and we spent Christmas Eve together and the next morning had egg sandwiches and coffee from the deli and I bought a Drake's honey bun as a holiday treat for myself. I'd never spent a Christmas away from home and was very sad. I missed the Michigan winter landscapes, the lake-effect snowstorms, the bitter cold air. I almost cried talking to my mom and Ed on the phone. Late in the day we went into the city. We looked at the tree at Rockefeller Center but it was too crowded and we didn't linger. We went to see The Thin Red Line at the Ziegfeld. A man behind us was crinkling a peanut bag.

Erin asked him politely to stop and the man lunged forward and got in her face and cursed her. She left the theater for several minutes and returned still upset. Meanwhile the movie had affected me strangely. It was a war movie, Terrence Malick's first film in twenty years. The pace was languid, the imagery often stunning, but I was overcome by a feeling of deepest dread. I went to the bathroom and my vision receded. I leaned into the sink to keep from fainting.

After the movie we walked down through Times Square and stopped at a food court for a snack. Two men next to us started screaming at each other and got in each other's faces and looked ready to take swings. Erin ran out. When I caught up to her she was standing on Broadway with tears in her eyes.

The sky was starless. The night was cold. The wind cut through our too-thin coats. We arrived at the party. It was a mellow scene. Paul knew some of the people. I only knew his friend Charles. I spent most of the night wandering back and forth between the living room and the kitchen, phasing in and out of various conversations. Shortly before midnight we gathered around the TV and counted down from ten as the ball dropped in Times Square. Everyone cheered. Paul and I hugged. There's something inside me, I know it. I want my life to be different. I want to achieve extraordinary things.

On the Thursday after New Year's Gina came to my desk.
—How would you feel about a little overtime?
—When?
—Tonight. I need you. Just for an hour or two. You see all these timesheets here and they just keep coming in.
I looked at the timesheets and then at the clock. It was almost five.
—You know I can't tonight. I already have plans.
Gina held my gaze for a moment and then turned to John.
—What about you?
—Actually I can't stay tonight either.
—Great. Thanks guys.
She shook her head and walked out of the room.

•

When I got home there was a message from my temp person saying my assignment had ended, no need to go in tomorrow. I called her back.

—What does that mean, my assignment has ended?

—It means your assignment's over.

—Yeah but why? I thought this was supposed to be a long-term thing.

—Apparently what, there was some overtime issue?

—Issue? No. I told her I didn't want to do it.

—Okay. Well. Could that have been the issue?

—I thought it was optional. She said how would you feel about overtime? How would you feel? Does that sound dire to you?

—Look all I know is I got a call from Gina saying don't send him back. It happens all the time. It's not a big deal.

—Not a big deal? How am I supposed to live?

—We'll get you something else.

—Okay. Today? Can you get me something today?

—Let me see what I have. I'll give you a call back tomorrow.

The next morning I called the Information Center.

—Gina it's Bryan. Please. Give me another chance.

—Bryan I'm sorry but I need someone in here I can count on. I mean you and that other guy, I had to get rid of him too.

—But I skipped Christmas. I stayed in New York for this job.

Silence.

—Gina listen to me. I have three hundred dollars.

She hung up. I stood there. Paul came in and suggested we go get breakfast. We walked to the Luncheonette Fountain and ate large platters of eggs and tasteless potatoes. When we returned the red light on the answering machine was blinking. It was a message for me from the head of the temp agency, a man with whom I'd had no prior dealings. He relayed to me in a borderline shout that I was way out of line calling his clients and I had no right to go telling tales out of school and the agency wouldn't be working with me anymore. I played the message again.

—That is amazing, said Paul.

He brought his four-track recorder into the kitchen, put a mic up to the answering machine and recorded the man's rant.

Erin's uptown sublet ended. She moved into a loft on Newel Street not far from my pad. Her room was okay but the people she lived with were struggling-musician creeps. The guy next door to her would hole up for hours playing the same idiotic funk bass line over and over again. I'd never known a musician of any kind who could work the same two-second riff so tirelessly. It was maddening.

One night I was lying on her bed contemplating all the things that were going wrong for me. I had no money and no job and no prospects. I'd finished another story and had sent it out but like the other one no one wanted it and the rejection slips were coming in.

—I know what'll make you feel better, she said.

—What?

—Put on your shoes, get your coat.

We turned left out of her building and walked to the end of the block. Across the street was a Key Food and a parking lot and a little cluster of fluorescent-lit shops. She led me through the parking lot into a Taco Bell Express. She ordered six regular hard-shell tacos, paid for them and we left. We ate them sitting on the floor of her room. She'd put on a CD to block out the dude's bass. It had been a long time since I'd had Taco Bell and the tacos were good.

—See don't you feel better?

—I really do.

I crunched another taco. She looked at me and laughed.

I called my mom but couldn't come right out with it. Late in the conversation she brought it up, asked how I was doing money-wise. I said I'd lost my temp job and things were bad. She offered to send me a check. I said I didn't want to put them out. She said You won't put us out. Ed got his big buyout check from GP and he has his pension coming in. No we're in good shape. She sent me a check for six hundred dollars. This brought me back up to eight hundred or so. I kept sending out resumés, ten or twelve at a time, barely keeping track of where I sent them anymore.

One Sunday there was an ad in the Times classifieds. Wanted: Marketing Writer was all it said. I faxed in my resumé and cover letter and the next day a man called and said he wanted to meet with me. His office was on John Street, not far from the law firm. I sat in a folding chair while he studied my resume. His mustache made bristling sounds as he stroked it.

—So Kalamazoo, Michigan huh? That's really a place?

—Yes it is.

—Funny. I thought it was just that old song.

—No. It's real.

He smiled. —Long way from home huh?

—Yeah I guess so.

—All right so lemme tell you a little bit about my client okay and then we'll talk and we'll see. They're a financial company, they're down here on Wall Street. And they're looking for someone with exactly these . . . qualifications.

The phone rang. The man answered it, spoke briefly, hung up.

—Sorry about that. So. Like I was saying, my client is a firm, a small mutual fund firm, they're over on Wall Street . . .

The man paused and searched my blank face.

—You uh. You know what a mutual fund is don't you?

—I have to be honest with you. I don't.

He sat back in his chair. He brushed at his mustache. He studied my resume.

—You know what, he said. —That's not a problem at all.

I took the train in early and stood on the corner of Water and Wall Street staring up at the building. I was wearing a suit I'd last worn at age fifteen. My mom had overnighted it to me for the sole purpose of this interview. Wall Street, she said, you're gonna wanna look sharp. But the suit was long out of fashion, if it had ever been fashionable in the first place—a big if. The jacket had weird useless buttons on it and now fit tightly everywhere. The sleeves stopped short of my wrists. The pants were too tight and the cuffs rose nearly to my shins when I sat. Over the suit I wore the battered maroon Carhartt I'd had since 1993. Frayed threads dangled from the sleeves and waist. On my feet were scuffed black Clarks and white tube socks. I crossed the street, went into the lobby and took the elevator to the twenty-third floor.

A woman named Clara met me in the reception area and led me back to her office. She studied my resumé. She looked at me and smiled.
 —So tell me about yourself.
 —Well uh. Let's see. I'm a writer. Um. I just moved here a few months ago—
 —That's your main interest, your passion? Writing?
 —My passion? Yeah I suppose it is.
 She leaned back in her chair. —I assume you know what we do here.
 —Well sure. Yes. I mean I have an idea.
 —An idea.
 —Yes.
 —You know what a mutual fund is?
 —I . . . vaguely. But it's like I explained to the g—
 —And you, let's see.
 She looked at my resumé. —You were a substitute teacher in— Portage? Teaching—sociology?
 —Sociology. Yes.
 —And you have no previous marketing experience, correct?
 —That's correct.
 I felt my face burning. I was uncomfortable in my suit. At the end of the interview she thanked me for coming and said they'd be in touch. I walked out of the building feeling shrunken and small. I'd written the whole thing off by the time I got home but the head-hunter called later and said Clara liked me. They wanted to see me again.

.

The following week I went back and sat in a large conference room taking a proofreading test. I turned it in with no hope or despair, figuring now I'd put Primary Funds out of my mind for good. It had been an interesting diversion but Wall Street wasn't my scene, that was clear. Surely there were other people in the running for the job who actually understood what the job entailed, people with business or marketing degrees. They'd weed me out now, they had to. Good thing I was honest with Clara and told her I didn't know shit. I could've gotten in over my head. Things could've gotten out of hand.

—You're on a roll, said the headhunter. —I guess you really nailed that test.

—I did?

—Apparently. They want you to come in again.

—They do?

—Yeah. Writing test this time.

—Huh. All right.

—You don't sound too thrilled.

—No I'm thrilled. But . . . another test?

—Yeah but this one's the big one. The writing test. See? You're applying for a job as a financial writer.

—No I know, I get it. It's just, things are getting a little tight here. I don't have a ton of time to play around with, financially speaking.

—Look. Hang in there okay. This looks promising. All you gotta do now is wow em with your writing skills. And that's easy, right?

I laughed. —I guess so.

—Hey. You made it this far.

I went back on a Friday late in the day. I'd been told Clara was out and that I'd be meeting a woman named Samantha. I sat in the waiting area and flipped through a financial magazine. The receptionist had left and the office seemed still and quiet from out there. She came around the corner. She looked about my age and had black hair and wore a black suit and was smiling and had a beautiful smile. I set the magazine on the table and rose and shook her outstretched hand.

—Hi. I'm Samantha.

She led me down a hall and into a large office. She gestured to a vacant desk in the corner. Next to the computer monitor was a yellow pad, a pen, and a sheet of paper with a single block of text printed on it.

—There's the assignment, she said.

I glanced at the paper and then back at her.

—You can use the computer there. You know how to turn it on?

I looked at it quickly. —Yeah. No problem.

—Anything else you need? Water or anything?

—No I think this should do it.

—Okay. Good luck.

She smiled and turned to leave and then paused and looked at her watch.

—I'm heading out right at five, I have to be somewhere. You can just leave your test on the front desk on your way out.

—The front desk. Got it.

I watched her walk out. The room buzzed with her presence. I still smelled her perfume. What are you doing here? Where do you have to be?

Two hours later I was sitting on the high barber-style chair next to the counter. Paul was at the stove frying burgers.

—I'm telling you it was jarring. One minute I'm staring at Financial Planner Weekly or some shit, the next minute this beautiful girl appears.

—That's how it is in New York. Think of all the beautiful women you see on the street. They all have to work somewhere.

—Yeah but there's something about this place. It just seemed unlikely.

—What was the writing test like?

—I had to write a brochure for a mutual fund.

—Do you know how to do that?

—No but another applicant's file was out on the desktop. I clicked it open and read it to kinda get some ideas.

The door opened. Craig walked in.

—Burger night, said Paul.

—Sweet. Can I have one?

—Sure.

Craig took his coat off and went to his room. He came back to the kitchen, washed his hands, formed a burger patty and put it in the pan.

—I'll make some corn. That way it'll be a complete meal.

Craig heated a can of Del Monte corn. He took a head of iceberg lettuce from the crisper, put a few pale leaves in a bowl and doused them with ranch.

—Anybody else want a salad?

Paul and I declined. The three of us brought our food to the living room and sat with our plates in our laps. We ate our burgers and watched TV.

Erin's birthday party was at a bar on the lower east side. A famous techno DJ and his pal, a hip painter, were there. The DJ was small and bald and I sat across from him feeling insecure and uncomfortable. His friend was saying something about a problem with the doorman asking to see some ID and he didn't have any on him. He said he should've just gone to the newsstand and bought a copy of Vogue and shown the doorman that, that would've proved he was twenty-one. I asked him why Vogue and he said there was a big spread on him in the current issue. More people arrived. I sat with Jonathan and Pete, a playwright and actor. I'd met them before and knew them a little but couldn't shake the feeling that I was beneath them somehow. One of Jonathan's plays was in an anthology I'd been assigned in a college playwriting class. Pete had a hilarious scene-stealing cameo in a well-known indie flick. The three of us drank and talked about books. Pete said he'd love to read some of my stuff. Yeah Charles, said Jonathan, what the fuck? I laughed it off. I changed the subject.

At the end of the night we took a cab back to Brooklyn. On the Williamsburg Bridge I turned and looked back and the city lights blinked like a billion earth-stuck stars and in the dark of her bedroom she bent down to kiss me and her hair fell around me and I moved into her and she sighed. I ran my hands over her legs up her waist to her breasts. I love you, I whispered. The words surprised and terrified and thrilled me. I didn't know if I meant them. I didn't know anything. Erin said my name. We moved together in the darkness.

The headhunter was on the phone again telling me they'd narrowed it down to just me and another guy. He said he'd let me know the minute he heard. I was floored. I never thought for a second I stood a chance at this job. Now that it was a possibility I couldn't think of anything else. I called back the next morning. Still no news. They waited another day and then made their offer. Thirty-two thousand a year plus full benefits. I said yes immediately without a word or even a thought of negotiation. I hung up and stood there, high on relief. Somehow I'd done it, I'd saved myself. And done it in high style. Thirty-two grand was some righteous coin, more than I ever thought I'd make. It's funny the things that change your life. A three-word want ad had delivered me to this precipice. I tumbled headlong and blindfolded over the edge.

The pilot said Flight attendants please prepare for takeoff. The engines revved. The plane sped down the runway. My hands were sweating and shaking, my heart was pounding, I struggled for breath. We left the earth and I turned and caught a glimpse of the city. The little towers of the World Trade Center in the distance under a gray winter sky.

Grocery Store

David Jaicks

Talking like a candidate, I walk into the grocery store. Nobody is around, so I step solidly onto a milk crate. We've got to forget about ourselves, slow down and drive slowly across the barrier.

Listen to the fury of our voices. Gaze carefully at the smooth sun. We must walk into the streams of conflict. Hold up our lives like they were swords with sharp and blazing blades.

We must rest and play in the leaves of the season. There we can be a part of the lives of our friends.

"The topic is to begin with is the topic at hand," I say quietly to a box of cereal. I am a candidate for the mayor of foodtown. The onions relax. The potatoes are in a fury.

We've got to put our best foot forward," I announce. The rafters holding signs begin to shade like a crowded stadium. "If you don't start now you might never begin," I say loudly standing high waving a flag.

Across the vegetables, I begin to see hands moving. People rising up, and celebrating my words. The eggs are ready to vote like dozens of bald men.

OPEN CITY

A woman runs up the aisle just to get a glimpse of me. Then inside the smoothness of my speech, I retire. Purchasing only a can of blueberries, I walk out.

Anagrams of Vision

Louise Despont

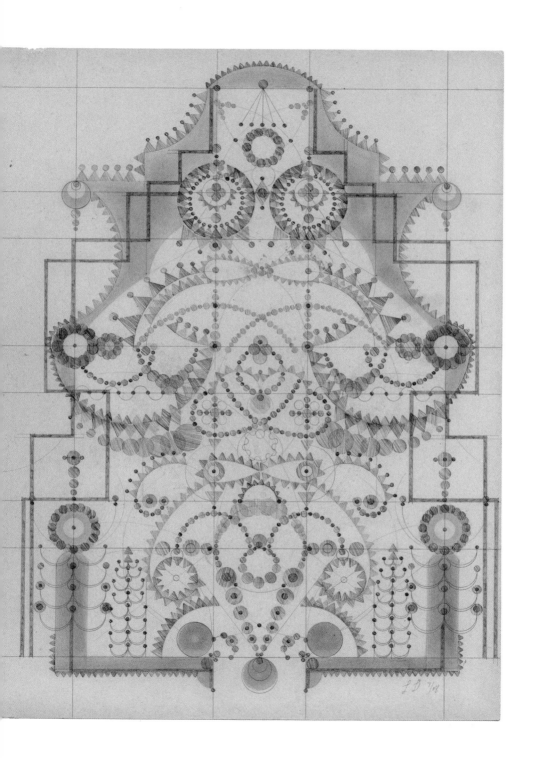

39 Gary Lippmans

Gary Lippman

Although no lovers, friends, or family came to his fortieth birthday party, all his younger selves turned up—all thirty-nine younger Garys, a Gary Lippman for each year, and the only ones he found that he could stomach were the kids; the rest of them, all so familiar, just made him see how little he's changed.

Lebenschluffen

"What's wrong," I asked the sunburnt man who lay on the sidewalk, and his answer—"I just can't take another step"—stirred something in me, gave me permission—Someone has acted on how I feel!—so I lay down beside the man, crossing my arms over my chest, and I gazed up at the bowl of sky, counting clouds and, after some time, getting sleepy.

Gary Lippman

A Prize Subject for Diane Arbus

Pointing her chin toward the hollow-eyed thin woman near us, my friend Gert whispered, "There's a subject for Diane Arbus," but because she whispers loudly—I've called her on this more than once!—the woman turned to Gert and said, "Actually, I *was*."

Two Ears of Rice

Although he'd loved her for all the decades they'd been married, the master origami artist shed no tears until five weeks after her death when he compared an ear of rice to his rendering of it and saw no difference between the two and for a moment felt like God but then recalled how weak he was with everything except for paper.

Gary Lippman

The Sound of Wine

Losing his patience with the wine steward—all the fuss the young man made—Baron Herzog took the bottle, poured a little on his palm, put the palm up to his ear, and told the steward, "You have to listen to sense its flavor."

Fill 'Er Up

Glenda said, "A lovely place, hmm?" to the woman who sat beside her at the opera, a tall, quite proper-looking woman who said, "It is, and you should see it when they fill this place with water."

Untitled

Stephen Campbell Sutherland

The goose-skin sticks out on account of the cold
pricks this Nov., the leaves gilt, not quite yet red.
Thinking of what to marry. You know,
my father would never have approved of you—
he wanted a Southerner, through and through—
not a goddamn I-Tie, Dago, Hun, any sort
of fair-weather foreigner that took my
earnest, youthful eye away; at one stage, reluctantly,
a "von" would do, but it was not to happen.
(And nor was it to be you.) Now I'm stuck
with suppositions, none correct, all black.
Each seems just as good as the next.
Our choices only as good as we who make them,
Jean is cooking day-old bones and scrambled eggs
for her itinerant mongrel, who demands a feast proper.

Legal Tape

This situation needs unraveling
Looks like I'm in it for the long-haul
Words have been said, recorded
Again and again and again
How much longer can it go on

How much longer can it go on
At this rate, a lot can linger
I just want to be rid of new evidence
As if it and you never existed
Then where do we go from here

Then where do we go from here
Bully-boy tactics have their appeal
I'll leave it / them in your capable hands
You know what's best for bigger interest
And, you know, I tried everything

And, you know, I tried everything
In our now respective favors
To get all right, correct by the books
The whole thing has gone quite wrong
Politics of the matter notwithstanding

Politics of the matter notwithstanding
And, you know, I tried everything
Then where do we go from here
How much longer can it go on
This situation needs unraveling

Stephen Campbell Sutherland

SATs

(1)
"Praetorian" is to the present Rome as "a classical education" is to . . .
willingness to pay thirty dinarii
a gladiator facing certain slavery
the abstruse shock of the new
the valour of examination

(2)
Your sex is to mine as a brand new shoot is to . . .
pedestrian versus cyclist
Irenaeus versus Darwin
how green leaves are to old trees
the valour of examination

(3)
Love is to hate as the map of the world is to...
Bartholomeo Columbus in the face of Amerigo Vespucci
Franklin in place of Theodore, Joseph instead of Winston
China against America (cf *The Little Red Book*)
the valour of examination

(4)
We are brought on this earth to pay . . .
God for putting us here
pray tell, a relinquishment of pain
homage to lip-service in duty
the valour of examination

(5)
The specter of death provides . . .
good knees-up revelry
the person you always wanted
a devil you don't know
an end to examination

24 hrs

I lay here unamused hence
   A Ramble in St. James's Park
Amongst leaves, no £s, but 50p.
   A Ramble in St. James's Park
How do you do you for me?
   A Ramble in St. James's Park
Your soul no match for Poverty
   A Ramble in St. James's Park
I'll make you over of Charity
   A Ramble in St. James's Park
And Chivalry, taught you blasphemy
   A Ramble in St. James's Park
And social climbing, you know now'n art
   A Ramble in St. James's Park
Whilst I sleep here, unpack my feak
   A Ramble in St. James's Park
What is it else you'd do for me?
   A Ramble in St. James's Park
Yr. Trickery mottled like Porphyryr
   A Ramble in St. James's Park
And now it sows no sense, of start
   A Ramble in St. James's Park
Here's where I'll sleep, here's where we part
   A Ramble in St. James's Park
You cry the whole time "suffer 'gain"
   A Ramble in St. James's Park
No man is wain, no girl in twain
   A Ramble in St. James's Park
For no length nor depth, no heart again's
   A Ramble in St. James's Park
Then why persist, with hate for art (thus art)
   A Ramble in St. James's Park

I wait the Rozzers come tonight
   A Ramble in St. James's Park
While German tourists, even, flourished
       (think of Marx, of Hess)
 A Ramble in St. James's Park
But all last summer, I took up no more fighting
   A Ramble in St. James's Park
You accuse me, were its me who's plighting
   A Ramble in St. James's Park
Stuck behind closed Gates, liv'ry all green in black
   A Ramble in St. James's Park
As were a stroll to sort the lack, and tack
   A Ramble in St. James's Park
Bright lights around, all going home to
   A Ramble in St. James's Park
Court: What else to tell you, then, to loll you
   A Ramble in St. James's Park
I recall a line: I love whilst thinking: That
 A Ramble in St. James's Park
Is, be, but, Jail, Jail, Jail, what. Goodnight
   A Ramble in St. James's Park
Be Bye, goodnight again, yet again. A good
Night in your heart, in my heart, as we part
We part wherever, how ever may be
Now.

Hyperion at X-mas

The seamless has shattered the over-
whelmed, over night, as it has over-
egged egos: to wit, witness, note
the "flight" of all small shops like
the once-all-mighty Cost Cutter
gone, expleted: these, exploited
by a Herodian birth, going, gone.

The whole Nazarene story –
the great girth of this, the cash-
mere New World Order style
offering, now offers bust. All
given up for you and yours truly
among the newly pensionless
to get lucky, or win the lottery.

Architectural Studies

Christopher de Lotbinière

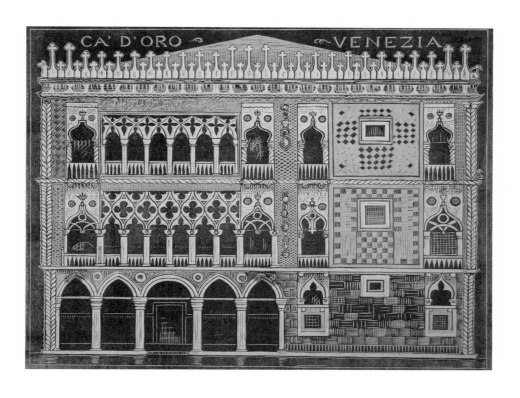

i. Palazzo Chiericati, Vicenza
ii. Chiesa di San Giorgio, Venice
iii. Ca' d'Oro, Venice
iv. Libreria Marciana, Venice
v. Chiesa di Santa Maria di Provenzano, Siena

Loophole Woman

Patricia Bosworth

I HAD BEEN AT *McCALL'S* MAGAZINE ONLY A FEW MONTHS AS
senior editor in charge of features when the galleys of Lois Gould's
Such Good Friends arrived on my desk.

It was 1970 in New York, and the Women's Liberation Movement
was at its height. I was attending meetings all over the city: sit-ins at
all-male bars, rallies against the Vietnam War, bra-burning marches,
abortion-rights vigils. Leaders—charismatic leaders like Gloria
Steinem and Bella Abzug—were emerging.

Every morning when I woke up, I felt a rush of excitement in the
air, and *Such Good Friends* was a part of that excitement because the
novel was the talk of publishing—this daring roman-à-clef about a
woman, Julie Messinger (said to be really Lois Gould), who discovers,
as her husband lies dying in a hospital, a coded diary of his many infidelities. There were frank descriptions in the novel of everything
from orgasms experienced to positions used, and dates and initials of
every mistress.

I sat up all night reading the book, impressed with the slashing,
quipping style that gave the prose enormous concentrated power.
The story was filled with such intense psychological cruelty and game
playing, it boggled the mind. And Julie Messinger took it all in
silence; it was quite astonishing, these descriptions of a paralysis so
profound as to keep many women in their place—immobile and in

pain as they try to hold marriage and family together while husbands merrily philander.

The next morning I phoned Lois. We knew each other from various protest groups. I told her I loved the novel and was going to get it reviewed. She seemed pleased. We made plans to have coffee the following week.

I subsequently assigned a terrific writer, Lucy Rosenthal, then the only female judge at the Book of the Month Club, to write the review. When it came in, it was a rave. I sent the review and the galleys as a matter of protocol to my boss, Shana Alexander, attaching a memo saying how important I thought the novel was, that it went along with the feminist rebelliousness of the times.

I waited for a reaction but none was forthcoming until about two weeks later, when Shana, who had recently been hired away from *Life* to energize the pages of *McCall's*, invited me to attend one of her staff luncheons, a ritual that featured "star guests" who were supposed to give the editors "fresh new ideas for the magazine." I soon learned the guests *du jour* would include Truman Capote, David Merrick, Arlene Francis, and former Senator Eugene McCarthy.

I can't remember many of the so-called "fresh ideas" that were brought up that afternoon. I think Arlene Francis suggested we review a movie called *Bonnie and Clyde* (I said we already had). Senator McCarthy was very concerned about Biafra—we should do a behind-the-scenes report on what was really going on with the food airlifts. Meanwhile, Truman Capote said nothing. He was a funny-looking little man with an enormous head set on a squat body. He appeared very hungover.

During a lull in the conversation, Shana suddenly held up the galleys of *Such Good Friends* and ordered me to explain why I'd chosen such a "filthy, obnoxious book to be reviewed by *McCall's*."

Although I was taken aback by her vehemence (Shana was a tiny, delicate blonde with a hesitant way of speaking), I managed to explain that I thought Lois Gould was writing a new kind of fiction, which one critic had already called "protest fiction," and that her novel was filled with irony, frustration, humiliation, all of it made bearable by her very dry wit. And, yes, she was angry at her husband's infidelities and she was angry because she had a giant need to be controlled by an authority figure. She had such a need, she didn't question her husband's right to use and humiliate her. All this *McCall's* readers would really relate to, as they did to other feminist novels of the period, such as Alix Kates Schulman's *Memoirs of an Ex-Prom Queen*.

With that, Shana, in a trembling voice, began reading from *Such Good Friends*; her selection recounted a sexual fantasy in which Julie performs fellatio on various men who give her nothing in return, after which she mocks herself: "Now, ladies and gents, the contract demands that Julie the Sword Swallower perform her world-famous teeth-grinding trick."

"I ask you," Shana demanded of Truman Capote, "would you recommend this novel to *McCall's* readers?

Capote murmured he'd never heard of the book, but after listening to that one paragraph he intended to go out and order it immediately!

As soon as the luncheon ended, Shana informed me that *Such Good Friends* would not be reviewed in *McCall's* under any circumstances. I attempted to argue for it, even enlisted others on the magazine to support me, but it did no good. Shana was the editor-in-chief, and she prevailed.

I was devastated. All the more so because I had to tell Lois. I phoned her, describing the lunch and the exchange with Capote. When I finished, she burst into delighted laughter. "Shana is taking it much too seriously!" she said, her voice cracking with amusement. "It's only a novel, for God's sake!"

I was too upset to respond. After a pause, Lois suggested we have a drink that evening. "I wanna cheer you up," she drawled.

Later, at the Plaza's Palm Court, against a background of wistful Cole Porter music, we proceeded to get quite drunk on a bottle of extremely good champagne. And we talked and talked. I soon realized Lois was more concerned about my emotional state of mind than she was about whether or not her novel was going to be reviewed.

Lois drew me out. We discovered we both had beautiful, control-ling mothers who were trying as hard as they could to make us feel worthless. That fact bonded us then and there. Then Lois changed the subject to careers. She told me that she'd been in magazines a lot longer than I had—indeed, she had been, until recently, executive editor of *Ladies' Home Journal*. So she was used to being "powerless in a powerful job."

What Shana had done was par for the course. As Lois said, "You had a good idea, she shot it down because she didn't think of it first, and also she might have been threatened by the content of the book. Who knows? The bottom line is you're going to have a lot of great ideas as an editor that are going to be shot down, and you better get used to that and just go on and don't take it personally and believe you won't be in magazines forever because they are a trap. They lead nowhere creatively. Eventually, you'll write if your dream is to be a writer." (I'd already confirmed it was.) She finished with, "You and I are loophole women."

"What is that?" I asked.

It was a phase she'd borrowed from Caroline Bird, who'd just writ-ten *Born Female—The High Cost of Keeping Women Down*. As far as Lois was concerned, "loophole women" were exceptions in a field where men were still in a majority of power positions: "We're hired to be exceptions, but we still have to toe the line. That's what Shana is doing, toeing the line. She's afraid to take a chance on my book." Which was too bad, since *Such Good Friends* soon garnered wonder-ful reviews all over the country and was widely read and then made into a big Hollywood movie directed by Otto Preminger.

In the next months, Lois and I found more opportunities to be together—we not only enjoyed each other's company but were both caught up in the movement. We joined a consciousness-raising group as well as two different writers' groups. It was an enormously exciting time.

I can still see Lois—moody, elegant, mysterious—drifting in and out of depression. For a while, she cut her hair short as a man's, wore a monocle, and flew to Rome to spend the summer writing a novel. For a while, she camped out in the shadowy loft she shared with her husband, the psychiatrist Robert Gould, who was as unconventional and strangely lovable as she.

Over the next twenty years, our friendship deepened, and the fears, doubts, conflicts, and persistent melancholy that simmered under Lois's formidable presence became clearer to me and contributed to my seeing her as a truly valiant creature.

In 1977, we were both active in a group called Women Against Pornography. Lois held many meetings in her loft. They often turned into shouting matches, because everybody had a different idea about how to define porn's dangers. I remember Lois serving cocktails and hors d'oeuvres before we marched on Times Square to protest the mainstreaming of violent hard-core porn up and down Forty-second Street.

Our antipornography campaign ultimately disintegrated in a tide of philosophical differences and name-calling. Lois was bitter about that. She thought this project was a true expression of radical feminism. She believed pornography was the synthesis of all violence against women's issues, including poverty, because women who get involved in the sex industry don't have many other economic options . . . and also included racism, because so many black and Asian women were stereotyped in *Hustler* and *Penthouse*. Eventually, Lois wrote a brilliant article about women and pornography for the *New York Times Magazine*.

Lois was tremendously productive at that time—dashing off essays and reviews and quirky original novels like *La Presidenta* (inspired by Eva Perón) and *Final Analysis*, a lethal satire about a woman in love with her ex-shrink. *A Sea Change* was her most ambitious radical work, a drama about vicious power plays and vulnerability, a story that rose to mythical proportions as Lois's heroine, in the process of getting rid of her weakness—her womanhood—harnesses her aggression and transforms herself into a man. It all takes place at the height of a raging hurricane, a storm so huge and forceful that the heroine sucks its power inside herself.

And then, in the middle 1980s (or was it the early 1990s?), Lois took off for Ireland, where she lived in a windswept castle for nearly five years, returning to New York periodically to see Bob, who waited patiently for her, and to be with her sons. By then, she told me, she felt undervalued by the world, felt she was being forgotten as a novelist. Never having been convinced that she was anything special, she longed for more recognition, but when her latest novel was praised to the skies, instead of promoting it around the U.S., she kept her potential celebrity at bay by staying in Europe.

We always kept in touch by letter and phone. Once, while I was struggling to write a memoir about my family, I told Lois I didn't want it to be "confessional." Lois almost snapped at me. "Don't use the word confessional!" she said. "You're having a confrontation with yourself!"

Lois died of cancer in 2002. Today it's hard to believe she's gone. Lois gave of herself with intense compassion, humor, and maternal tenderness, the kind of maternal tenderness she never received from her mother.

At her memorial, nobody talked enough about the impact her novels had made during the 1970s. Her books comprise part of a new genre, a protest fiction filled with women's contradictions and concerns. For Lois, the subtext was always the same, that the power of feminism lies in its capacity to transform women's consciousness at the deepest possible level.

I count myself lucky to have been one of Lois Gould's friends.

Porcini

Tomaž Šalamun

How do you germinate the lamb, the plucked-off neck, watered by milk?
Slovenians, with my tongue I touched your children's palm
and pressed their brains like muscat wine. I give you

back your home. If I pluck off their arms, they come after
them. The torso is my fountain of delight. I roll up
shirt sleeves: Perceval. White knouts with silky

edges are at your disposal. Christ's heart has to be
massaged. I grabbed Christ's heart with my fingers.
With the hand I licked by myself. Will the blossom now be

double, Marko? Can you hear the mushrooms grow? I know
you were rooted out, dethreaded, grabbed, and milled.
Your heart's sequins goggled. You were blown up.

Wet and moist, you screamed. Your little teeth
gave you a drink. The blueness scrubbed you as with sand.
You plucked out your hair and put it in the herbarium.

Diphtheria. Music's swarm. A ram's head covered with
zinc. Little bags. Little pouches that you can hide
bellow your armpit. The yellow beak of the blackbird itself.

Found as a fossil. To be of use? Did you cut them?
All one hundred and three of them support you. I'm only drawing.
I'm only drawing. The ball which runs on my biceps.

Spring Street

I had a sweet liver. Coasts to the sky.
Honking of the truck on Houston Street,
the dark one.

The tribe demolished the layer cake.
The layer cake destroyed the seed.
Salt. Midgets. I bite your white white bridge.

You sleepy, softly turned the wheel.
As a winch pulling a boat to earth,
you lift, you wreck my veins.

Let it flow into you, let it flow into you, my sweet juice.
You need me. If not, you wouldn't tear me apart.
You wouldn't move your warm

bread wrapped in rags.
For you yourself are pinned together, for me you crunch.
The sea of blood is not aware of the heat of your heart.

And cunning. But you don't know how
rich. Carried toward your bite-mark.
Spend. You froth, you froth,

Tomaž Šalamun

red blood breaks into a waterfall.
O leaf of my tree,
white fire of my grief.
You are seized,

my son, you are seized.
You flow away on the path
from which you came.

Translated from the Slovenian by Joshua Beckman and the author.

Harold Brodkey: The Great Pretender

Edmund White

A TALL, BLOND BIOLOGIST NAMED DOUG GRUENAU, FOUR YEARS younger than I but like me a graduate from the University of Michigan, was living with the novelist Harold Brodkey on West Eighty-eighth Street.

Harold had an immense underground reputation—which sounds like a contradiction in terms. Everyone in New York was curious about him, but few people outside the city had ever heard of him. Long ago, in 1958, he'd published *First Love and Other Sorrows*, a book of stories that had been well reviewed, but they weren't what all the buzz was about. Now he'd bring out a story occasionally in *The New Yorker* or *New American Review* or even *Esquire*. The one in *New American Review* (a quarterly, edited by Ted Solotaroff, which had once brought out a dirty chapter from Phillip Roth's *Portnoy's Complaint*) was highly sexual but not dirty—a fifty-page chapter, published in 1973, about a Radcliffe girl's first orgasm. The prose in "Innocence" could be strained if striking: "To see her in sunlight was to see Marxism die." It seemed the longest sex scene in history, rivaled only by the gay sex scene in David Plante's *The Catholic*—and reminiscent of the sex scene, "The Time of Her Time," included in Norman Mailer's *Advertisements for Myself* (except that one had been anal!). Then there had been troubled, labyrinthine stories about Brodkey's mother in *The New Yorker* of a length and complexity no one else would have gotten away with. This was obviously a writer, we thought, who must be, above all, extremely convincing. The mother stories nagged and tore at their subject matter with a Lawrentian exasperation, a relentless drive to get it right, repeatedly correcting the small assertions just made in previous lines. Everyone was used to confessional writing of some sort (though the heyday for that would come later) and everyone knew all about the family drama, but no one had ever gone this far with sex, with mother and with childhood. We were stunned by this new kind of realism that made slides of every millimeter of the past and put them under the writer's microscope. In *Esquire* in 1975, Brodkey published a short, extremely lyrical story, "His Son, in His Arms, in Light, Aloft," about a baby boy being carried in his father's arms. Mother might get the niggling, Freudian treatment, but Daddy deserved only light-drenched, William Blake-like mysticism.

All these "stories," apparently, were only furtive glimpses of the massive novel that Brodkey had been working on for years and that would be the American answer to Marcel Proust. Brodkey's fans (and there were many of them) Xeroxed and stapled into little booklets every story he'd published so far in recent years and circulated them among their friends, a sort of New York samizdat press. His supporters made wide fervent claims for him. Harold was our Thomas Mann, our James Joyce. That no one outside New York knew who he was only vouchsafed his seriousness, his cult stature, too serious for the unwashed (or rather the washed, a more appropriate synecdoche for Midwesterners like me).

He and Doug lived in a big, rambling West Side apartment with a third man, named Charlie Yordy, whom I met just once but who reeked of a hoofed and hairy-shanked sexuality. He was a friendly, smiling man but seemed burdened, as all people possessed by a powerful sexuality are.

Harold was as bearded and hooded-eyed as Nebuchadnezzar but tall and slim and athletic as well. He must have been in his forties. His constant swimming and exercising at the Sixty-third Street Y (the one I'd lived in when I first came to New York) kept him as fit as a much younger man. His moods and thoughts were restless, rolling about like ship passengers in a storm. Sometimes he looked as if a migraine had just drawn its gray, heavy wing across his eyes. The next moment he'd be calculating something silently, feverishly to himself—then he'd say out loud, "Forget it." Cryptic smiles flitted across his face. He seldom paid attention to what the people around him were saying because he was concocting his next outrage—for most of his remarks were outrageous, and he could not be cajoled out of them.

Harold had lived with Doug for some eight or nine years. Doug was so polite and respectful that even whenever Harold would say something absurdly farfetched, Doug would cock his head to one side and up a bit, as if he were a bird trying to make sense of a new, higher, quicker call. Doug was a big man with a bass laugh but around Harold he didn't take up much space. I think he'd decided that Harold was both cracked and a genius and that even his insults were, ultimately, harmless, but Doug taught biology in a private school and had endless hours of grading and preparation and counseling and teaching to do, whereas Harold appeared to have enough money to be idle—and to meddle. When I told David Kalstone about Harold, David sang, "Time on my hands . . ."

I wasn't quite sure what Charlie did, though I must have been told(Americans are never reluctant to ask strangers what they do). I think he was a math teacher and then he manufactured clothes in the Adirondacks. He wasn't around often, and in any event he seemed to be more Harold's boyfriend than Doug's, though I'm sure Harold told me they were all three lovers. The apartment was big enough to accommodate them all and even give each one of them privacy. Harold was on the prowl. Not all the considerable amount of time he spent at the Y was devoted to swimming. People who knew who he was said he was a tireless, overt cruiser.

Harold seldom talked about his own work but he loved to deliver pronouncements about literature and how to make it. He particularly enjoyed giving other writers—even older, more successful writers— advice. As the years went by I kept hearing strange and then stranger stories about him. One of his great defenders was Gordon Lish, a top editor at Knopf and the man who had virtually invented minimalism. Gordon apparently walked into the office of his boss, Bob Gottlieb (who'd started his own career as the editor of *Catch-22*, and had even been the one to persuade Joseph Heller to change the title from *Catch-18*), and said something like, "You've published a few good books, Bob, but nothing that will make people remember you after you're gone. Now you have the chance to publish Proust—but you must write a check for a million dollars and not ask to see even a single page."

At that point Harold had been signed up with Farrar, Straus for years, but they'd paid him a considerably smaller sum—and they weren't willing to give him the full attention he demanded. Harold needed not one editor but several to go over with him the thousands of pages he'd already written. As far as anyone could tell, he was years away from delivering. But their reluctance to put the full resources of their staff at his disposal roiled in Harold. Responding to the challenge, Gottlieb wrote the check.

In a slow groundswell of media attention leading up to publication, various magazine articles appeared about Harold, all wildly laudatory. I remember one in *Esquire* in 1977 by the religious novelist D. Keith Mano ("Harold Brodkey: The First Rave"), who confessed he'd set out to debunk Harold and his myth but who'd stayed to be conquered. Mano even told Brodkey about some of his personal problems—a minor betrayal by a friend. The passage is worth quoting because it reveals one of Harold's seduction techniques:

> . . . In passing I mention a personal misfortune, a betrayal—none of your business what—that had shocked and demoralized me the day before. Harold listens, advises; he parses it out. I hang up feeling both presumptuous and stupid. What am I to Harold Brodkey, he to me, that I should lay my tsuris on him? Yet, one hour later, Harold calls back. My distress, a stranger's distress, has alarmed him. We talk for thirty minutes on Harold's long-distance dime. The man cares. I am moved: such concern is unlooked-for. Subsequently, we talk several times. In fact I became, well, jealous; his stamina, his integrity, his

grasp of circumstances is better than mine and these, dammit, are my circumstances. After a while I'd prefer to forget; it's human enough. But Harold won't sanction that; his moral enthusiasm is dynamic; he knows I'm copping out. And I feel understood, seen through, swept into the rational and oceanic meter of his fiction. A Brodkey character. Me. Imagine.

Denis Donaghue and Harold Bloom had both compared Harold to Proust. Bloom, after reading some of Harold's new novel in manuscript, added that he was "unparalleled in American prose fiction since the death of William Faulkner." Cynthia Ozick declared him to be a true artist. Harold concurred: "I'm not sure that I'm not a coward. If some of the people who talk to me are right, well, to be possibly not only the best living writer in English, but someone who could be the rough equivalent of a Wordsworth or a Milton, is not a role that a halfway-educated Jew from St. Louis with two sets of parents and a junkman father is prepared to play."

The press response to his work (always by straight men) was so extreme that I developed a theory about what was behind it. I figured that gay men were not competitive in the way straights were; it was no accident that gays played individual not group sports. Nor were gay men awed by and half in love with their fathers. Most gays I knew had rejected their fathers and despised them. Finally, gays were thoroughly disabused and especially suspicious of flattery—more likely to hand it out than to take it in. As a result, Harold's methods didn't work on them (on me), but they instantly seduced straights. Harold would suddenly announce to a straight admirer (or adversary), "You know, Tom, you could be the greatest writer of your generation. There's no doubt about it. And by the way I'm not the only one to think that." Long pause. "But you won't be—wanna know why?" Strong eye contact. "Because you're too damn lazy. And too damn modest. You don't work hard enough or aim high enough."

His interlocutor, after having his rank raised as high as it was in his most secret dreams, suddenly saw his hopes dashed, unless . . . unless . . .

He suddenly needed Harold to help him, to inspire him, finally to judge him. Harold was his father/coach, while the challenger was the son/rookie. With any luck he might yet emerge as the world-class genius he dreamed of being.

Bitchy and disagreeable as gays are sometimes thought to be, they don't usually play lethal games like these. They don't try to mold behavior—perhaps they (we) aren't confident enough to challenge another man in his heart of hearts, the private interior place where he lives. We gays don't want to belong, we don't want to play ball—we're not team players, so how could we bow before someone evaluating us? We'd rather lose, quit the playing field—be a quitter. How can our father or father's brother bully us when we're all too ready to cry uncle? That sort of ducking-out is our way of winning.

Of course it probably helped that Harold went to almost every literary party and spent hours on the phone every day with Don DeLillo, Harold Bloom, Denis Donoghue. DeLillo told him the way to stop worrying about death was to watch a lot of television.

The funny thing is that no one ever mentioned that Harold lived with not one but two men and that he was notorious in the YMCA steam room. Harold was not known to be gay—and he was far from a cool, impersonal writer. His whole life's work was based on his childhood and adolescent experiences. He had turned himself into a tall, complicated, handsome, athletic, brilliant Jewish lad, and that's how everyone who didn't know him personally perceived him.

Harold had raised expectations so high—after all, he wasn't just trying to "get a second book out," he was writing the great American novel—that of course he had to introduce roadblocks in his own path. He bought a computer. But this was still the era when a computer filled a whole room, when only industries and spies owned them, when one had to master a whole new method of writing, of programming. Harold invited me to see the machines humming and buzzing in one room, which someone from IBM was teaching him, day after day, week after week, how to operate. The entire long, sprawling manuscript would have to be transferred to the computer. Only then could it be properly analyzed for content, repetitions, inner consistency and flow.

My heart sank, I who still scribbled with a ballpoint in students' notebooks. I rewrote but quickly, only once; it was the least demanding part of composition and by far the most pleasant. Much of my rewriting was cutting. I also liked to plant early on foreshadowing of later plot developments, just as once I'd finished a first draft I went back over my manuscript to set up echoes of themes and imagery, little sleights-of-hand that would make the finished book appear to be more unified. For me rewriting was fun, quick, a way of painting with a wet brush to give the whole an impression of speed and virtuosity. All those conceits that had become leaden were just crossed out. All those tales within tales were unboxed and streamlined into one forward movement. I was convinced I was a good editor of my own work and I enjoyed rectifying my mistakes.

What was hard for me was composing, writing. I had so little confidence or stamina that a single paragraph could send me into a paroxysm of self-doubt. Sometimes I felt I was blasting my way through a sheer wall of granite, forcing a small path through vast thick ramparts of low self-esteem and resistance. At other times I felt I was racing through the woods but that the trail had given out, was overgrown—or had broke into two paths or three. I had no idea where to go, no momentum, no sense of direction.

Harold appeared to have none of these doubts. He sometimes spoke of writing in a way that reminded me of the methods discussed by French writers. A French author might say that he'd worked the whole book out in his mind, done his research, constructed the whole intrigue—and now all he had to do was the "redaction," by which he would mean the actual writing, as if that were a detail, the way some composers refer to the orchestration. I was never shown any of the manuscript in all its voluminousness, but I would get vague, haggard battle reports about how the organization was going.

I think you could have called Harold a phenomenologist. He once said to me (à propos of some of my own writing), "When someone writes, 'She went down on him,' it's always a lie." His idea was that shorthand expressions (going down on someone) were smug and false because the real experience (of sucking or being sucked) is so profound, so unrepeatable, so thick with emotions and half-thoughts and fears and tremblings that the only expression adequate to it is minute, precise, original, and exhaustive. In print Harold wrote: "I distrust summaries, any kind of gliding through time, any too great a claim that one is in control of what one recounts."

Perhaps because it suited my own artistic temperament, I learned from Harold to "de-familiarize" the world and to render it in the freshest, most Martian way possible. Where I disagreed with him was that I thought not everything could be treated so thoroughly. There had to be background and foreground, and what was in the background necessarily should be sketched in—not with clichés but with some familiarity, even facility.

If that was the most sensible and useful part of Harold's advice, he was also capable of strange little obsessions. In reading a description of mine of a skylight above a library (one which happened to be installed in a nineteenth-century opera house), Harold insisted that I describe the overhead windows as an eye. I didn't think it made much difference in a book of two hundred twenty pages whether I used that metaphor or not, but I quickly acceded to his demand to humor him and to show him that I was flattered that he had had a concrete suggestion of any sort. Presumably he had read the rest of the book (it was *A Boy's Own Story*) but he made no comment on the other 219 pages.

When my book was in the proof stages he called my editor, Bill Whitehead, and said, "Stop the presses! White has stolen my style." Bill, who could be very firm, said, "That's nonsense—he wouldn't want your style and anyway a style can't be patented," and hung up on him. Harold kept calling back, threatening legal action, but he seldom contacted me and Bill never again took his calls. Harold also accused John Updike of stealing his personality. "I am the Devil in *The Witches of Eastwick*," Harold announced.

The years went by and Harold threatened to publish his book. Sometimes it was said to be 2,000 pages long and sometimes it was said he'd written between 3,000 and 6,000 pages. The most famous fashion photographer in the world, Richard Avedon, told me that he was collaborating with Harold since he was convinced he was America's greatest author. Harold wrote the introduction to a book of

Avedon's photos taken between 1947 and 1977, an essay that had the distinction of being both laborious and stylish. The title of his novel changed from *Party of Animals* to *The Runaway Soul*, i.e., from a striking title to a forgettable one. It was reported he'd gone back from Knopf to Farrar, Straus. As the new high-priest of heterosexuality and the female orgasm, he had no need of the embarrassing evidence to the contrary that Doug Gruenau and Charlie represented. Charlie had already moved out with a new lover in 1975 and Doug left the apartment in 1980. Harold moved a woman in—Ellen Schwamm, a writer he'd met while jogging in the park. (There are other versions of how they'd met. In one, Ellen asked Gordon Lish who was the greatest living writer and when she found out it was Harold she set her cap for him. In another they met at a bookstore, the then fashionable Books & Co. next to the Whitney). Ellen and Harold cut their hair so that they would resemble each other, like the couple in Hemingway's posthumously published and thrillingly good *The Garden of Eden*. She had left her rich husband for Harold. Charlie was an early victim of AIDS and died. Doug found a new lover and remained friendly with Harold and Ellen, though was never to be mentioned in the press. I tried to date Doug but he was too sweet, too genuine for me—and besides he didn't smoke, he took long hikes in the desert to photograph bison and got up every morning at six to go jogging around the reservoir. With any luck I was just rolling into bed at that hour, putting out my seventy-second cigarette of the day. I felt sooty and superficial next to Doug—and soon he found a serious lover he's still with after these many years.

I kept hearing nutty reports about Harold. He'd accepted a job teaching the occasional semester at Cornell. Alison Lurie, who taught there, told me that Harold had accused a sweet elderly novelist, James McConkey, of climbing across several roofs and slipping like a cat burglar into Harold's room in Ithaca in order to copy out long passages of Harold's novel and to publish them as his own. There was a tremendous row that in a more sensible century would have ended in a simplifying duel instead of the mess that went on for years.

Susan Sontag told me about her evening with Harold. He had said to her, "You and I, Susan, are the greatest writers of the twentieth century." She had replied, "Oh really, Harold? Aren't there a few others? What about Nabokov, for instance."

"Oh he's nothing," Harold said, "but at least he had the decency to acknowledge his debt to me."

"Really, Harold? Where did he do that?"

As though slowing down and simplifying things for a child, Harold took a breath and smiled and said, "You remember that at the beginning of *Lolita* that Lolita has a father who's already died?"

"Yes . . ."

"And do you remember his first name?"

"Yes, his name is Harold."

Harold shrugged—case closed. Harold seemed seriously to believe that his stories in *First Love and Other Sorrows* had inspired Nabokov—another instance of his style being stolen.

The writer Sheila Kohler told me that when she had dinner with Harold she told him that she was happy to meet him since Gordon Lish had said he was the greatest living writer. "Why, he compares you to Shakespeare," she told Harold.

Harold looked at her balefully and said, "I bet he wouldn't put Shakespeare on hold." Harold suggested that for this grievous insult he was considering changing publishers yet again.

C. K. Williams, the Pulitzer prize–winning poet, one of the sweetest and most talented men of Harold's generation, was introduced to him by Avedon, but rather quickly Harold fought with him. Harold accused him of pilfering some of his pages to put into a poem—though later Harold realized that Williams could never have seen those pages since they hadn't yet been published. For once in his life Harold apologized.

And then the *The Runaway Soul* came out and it was a terrible flop. James Wood, even though he was defending it, called it "microscopically narcissistic." Pages we'd once admired in the *New Yorker* were now so bent out of shape through rewriting as to be incomprehensible. No one could follow the action. Hundreds of pages went by and we were still mired in earliest childhood—and Harold's insights and observations seemed utterly implausible. No one had that kind of detailed recall about what happened when he was two or three.

Piaget had demonstrated that even if we were given complete access to our infant memories they would make no sense to us since they were inscribed in a different, earlier language than the one we think in now. And, anyway, who cared? It was all the fault, I thought, of that infernal computer and Harold's infinitely expanded opportunities to rewrite. The book was no longer a performance but a smudged palimpsest.

Once his masterpiece went belly up in such a conspicuous and unresounding way, Harold filled his days more usefully by writing bits and pieces for "The Talk of the Town." He was a good journalist, good at getting the story and willing to curb his eccentric style enough to communicate to the average educated reader. Apparently he wrote TV pilots for money as well.

Then one day Harold wrote a short piece in the *New Yorker* announcing he had AIDS and was dying. Apparently—or so Harold claimed—he'd been infected in the 1960s, since that was the last time he'd fooled around with a man. I wondered how Doug reacted to this denial of all their many years together. I thought, only Harold could write a page and a half about his imminent death from AIDS and manage to irritate the reader.

He wrote a strangely homophobic book about his AIDS, *This Wild Darkness: The Story of My Death*. He claimed that the book was born of a decision to be honest, not to lie, but in fact he obscured many of the facts. He never mentioned Doug Gruenau or his countless tricks. He acted as if his major contact with Charlie Yordy was based on the fact that they were both orphans (Harold's parents died when he was very young). He claimed that his affair with Charlie (which in the book sounds like his only gay relationship) was a way of re-living the childhood trauma of being sexually abused by his stepfather. As an adult, he said, he had "experimented with homosexuality to break my pride, to open myself to the story" of being abused as a child. This experience may have helped Harold to come to terms with being repeatedly raped but, as Harold goes on to say, "I think he was the one who gave it to me," i.e. AIDS. In the gay community it had been decided early on that it wasn't kosher to try to pinpoint the one who'd infected us. Hurling accusations of that sort was a waste of breath—especially since Harold, like the rest of us, had had not one but hundreds of male partners.

When Harold died it felt anticlimactic. He was obviously a brilliant if underemployed and meddling man. He had great natural gifts and more than a touch of madness. His own wife (Ellen was his second wife—he'd been married to a magazine editor when he was young and had an adult daughter from that union) had written a novel (the ironically titled *How He Saved Her*) in which Harold appeared as the devil, destroying everyone around him. He died nearly the same day as the more famous Russian poet Joseph Brodsky and had the misfortune of being confused with him in many people's minds. Now he's been practically forgotten—and the loss of this large, ambitious talent seems tragic. We all wanted him to be a success. It's more fun to have a genius in our midst. Now we had to be content with just Balanchine.

Open City Index (Issues 1–27)

Badanes, Jerome. "The Man in the Twelve Thousand Rooms" (essay). *Open City* 23 (2007): 1–3.

Badanes, Jerome. "Guinea Golden," "From Day to Day," "Late Night Footsteps on the Staircase" (poems). *Open City* 23 (2007): 5–10.

Bakowski, Peter. "The Width of the World," "We Are So Rarely Out of the Line of Fire" (poems). *Open City* 11 (2000): 95–100.

Balkenhol, Stephan. Drawings. *Open City* 5 (1997): 38–42.

Bar-Nadav, Hadara. "Talking to Strangers" (story). *Open City* 23 (2007): 11–23.

Bar-Nadav, Hadara. "Bricolage and Blood," "I Used to Be Snow White," "To Halve and to Hole" (poems). *Open City* 23 (2007): 25–29.

Bartók-Baratta, Edward. "Walker" (poem). *Open City* 18 (2003–2004): 175.

Batlle, Jay. "People Like This Hate People Like You" (drawings). *Open City* 24 (2007–2008): 119–124.

Baum, Erica. "The Following Information" (photographs). *Open City* 13 (2001): 87–94.

Baumbach, Jonathan. "Lost Car" (story). *Open City* 22 (2006): 27–35.

Baumbach, Jonathan. "Travels with Wizard" (story) *Open City* 24 (2007–2008): 125–136.

Baumbach, Nico. "Guilty Pleasure" (story). *Open City* 14 (2001–2002): 39–58.

Beal, Daphne. "Eternal Bliss" (story). *Open City* 12 (2001): 171–190.

Beatty, Paul. "All Aboard" (poem). *Open City* 3 (1995): 245–247.

Becker, Priscilla. "Blue Statuary," "Instrumental" (poems). *Open City* 18 (2003–2004): 151–152.

Becker, Priscilla. "Recurrence of Childhood Paralysis," "Blue Statuary" (poems). *Open City* 19 (2004): 33–34.

Becker, Priscilla. "Typochondria" (essay). *Open City* 22 (2006): 9–12.

Becker, Priscilla. "Math Poem," "Midwestern," "afters," "Desert," "Hatred of Men with Blonde Eyebrows" (poems). *Open City* 26 (2008–2009): 15–20.

Beckman, Joshua and Tomaž Šalamun, trans., "VI," "VII" (poems) by Tomaž Šalamun. *Open City* 15 (2002): 155–157.

Beckman, Joshua and Tomaž Šalamun, trans.,"Porcini," "Spring Street" (poems) by Tomaž Šalamun. *Open City* 27 (2009):147–150 .

Beckman, Joshua and Matthew Rohrer. "Still Life with Woodpecker," "The Book of Houseplants" (poems). *Open City* 19 (2004): 177–178.

Belcourt, Louise. "Snake, World Drawings" (drawings). *Open City* 14 (2001–2002): 59–67.

Bellamy, Dodie. "From *Cunt-Ups*" (poems). *Open City* 14 (2001–2002): 155–157.

Beller, Thomas. "Vas *Is* Dat?" (story). *Open City* 10 (2000): 51–88.

Bellows, Nathaniel. "At the House on the Lake," "A Certain Dirge," "An Attempt" (poems). *Open City* 16 (2002–2003): 69–73.

Bowes, David. Illustrations for Carlo McCormick's "The Getaway." *Open City* 3 (1995): 150–154.

Bowers, William. "It Takes a Nation of Millions to Hold Us Back" (story). *Open City* 17 (2003): 67–69.

Bowles, Paul. "17 Quai Voltaire" (story). *Open City* 20 (2005): 223–229.

Bowman, Catherine. "I Want to Be Your Shoebox," "Road Trip" (poems). *Open City* 18 (2003–2004): 75–79.

Boyers, Peg. "Transition: Inheriting Maps" (poem). *Open City* 17 (2003): 163–165

Bradley, George. "Frug Macabre" (poem). *Open City* 4 (1996): 223–237.

Branca, Alba Arikha. "Yellow Slippers" (story). *Open City* 3 (1995): 81–88.

Branca, Alba. "A Friend from London" (story). *Open City* 9 (1999): 43–52.

Brannon, Matthew. "The Unread Unreadable Master of Overviolence" (bookmark). *Open City* 16 (2002–2003): 119–120.

Bridges, Margaret Park. "Looking Out" (story). *Open City* 6 (1998): 47–59.

Broun, Bill. "Heart Machine Time" (story). *Open City* 11 (2000): 111–118.

Brown, Erin. "Reckoning" (story). *Open City* 24 (2007–2008): 99–102.

Bao, Quang. "Date" (poem). *Open City* 8 (1999): 137–140.

Brown, Jason. "North" (story). *Open City* 19 (2004): 1–19.

Brown, Lee Ann. "Discalmer" (introduction). *Open City* 14 (2001–2002): 137–139.

Brownstein, Michael. "The Art of Diplomacy" (story). *Open City* 4 (1996): 153–161.

Brownstein, Michael. "From *World on Fire*" (poetry). *Open City* 14 (2001–2002): 201–218.

Broyard, Bliss. "Snowed In" (story). *Open City* 7 (1999): 22–42.

Brumbaugh, Sam. "Safari Eyes" (story). *Open City* 12 (2001): 49–64.

Bukowski, Charles. "The Silver Christ of Santa Fe" (story). *Open City* 25 (2008): 63–68.

Bunn, David. "Book Worms" (card catalog art project). *Open City* 16 (2002–2003): 43–57.

Burton, Jeff. "Untitled #87 (chandelier)" (photograph). *Open City* 7 (1999): front cover.

Butler, Robert Olen. "Three Pieces of *Severance*" (stories). *Open City* 19 (2004): 189–191.

C, Mark. "What Calls Your Name" (photographs). *Open City* 25 (2008): 137–146.

Carter, Emily. "Glory Goes and Gets Some" (story). *Open City* 4 (1996): 125–128.

Carter, Emily. "Hampden City" (story). *Open City* 7 (1999): 43–45.

Cattelan, Maurizio. "Choose Your Destination, Have a Museum-Paid Vacation" (postcard). *Open City* 9 (1999): 39–42.

Cavendish, Lucy. "Portrait of an Artist's Studio" (drawings). *Open City* 11 (2000): 101–110.

Daniels, René. "Paintings, 1977–1987" (paintings). *Open City* 14 (2001–2002): 187–194.

Dannatt, Adrian. "After a Giselle Freund Photograph," "Utrecht" (poems). *Open City* 2 (1993): 126–127.

Dannatt, Adrian. Introduction to "The House Where I Was Born." *Open City* 7 (1999): 112–115.

Dannatt, Adrian. "Days of Or" (story). *Open City* 8 (1999): 87–96.

Dannatt, Adrian. "Central Park Wet" (story). *Open City* 10 (2000): 103–114.

Dannatt, Trevor. "Night Thoughts (I)," "Night Thoughts (II)" (poems). *Open City* 19 (2004): 133–134.

Daum, Meghan. "Inside the Tube" (essay). *Open City* 12 (2001): 287–304.

David, Stuart. "A Peacock's Wings" (story). *Open City* 13 (2001): 133–138.

Davies, Howell. "The House Where I Was Born" (story). *Open City* 7 (1999): 116–119.

Deller, Jeremy. "The English Civil War (Part II)" (photographs). *Open City* 9 (1999): 159–166.

Delvoye, Wim. Drawings, text. *Open City* 2 (1993): 39–42.

DeMarinis, Rick. "The Life and Times of a Forty-Nine Pound Man" (story). *Open City* 17 (2003): 185–196.

Dermont, Amber. "Number One Tuna" (story). *Open City* 19 (2004): 95–105.

Despont, Louise. "Anagrams of Vision" (drawings). *Open City* 27 (2009): 113–122.

Dezuviria, Sacundo. Photograph. *Open City* 2 (1993): back cover.

Dietrich, Bryan D. "This Island Earth" (poem). *Open City* 16 (2002–2003): 201–202.

Dietrich, Bryan D. "The Thing That Couldn't Die" (poem). *Open City* 21 (2005–2006): 89–90.

Dikeou, Devon. Photographs, drawings, and text. *Open City* 1 (1992): 39–48.

Dikeou, Devon. "Marilyn Monroe Wanted to Be Buried In Pucci" (photographs, drawings, text,). *Open City* 10 (2000): 207–224.

Donnelly, Mary. "Lonely" (poem). *Open City* 12 (2001): 151–152.

Doris, Stacy. "Flight" (play). *Open City* 14 (2001–2002): 147–150.

Dormen, Lesley. "Gladiators" (story). *Open City* 18 (2003–2004): 155–163.

Douglas, Norman. "Male Order" (story). *Open City* 19 (2004): 151–163.

Dowe, Tom. "Legitimation Crisis" (poem). *Open City* 7 (1999): 21.

Doyle, Ben. "And on the First Day" (poem). *Open City* 12 (2001): 203–204.

Duhamel, Denise. "The Frog and the Feather" (story). *Open City* 5 (1997): 115–117.

Dyer, Geoff. "Albert Camus" (story). *Open City* 9 (1999): 23–38.

Grennan, Eamon. "Two Poems" (poems). *Open City* 5 (1997): 137–140.

Eisenegger, Erich. "A Ticket for Kat" (story). *Open City* 16 (2002–2003): 133–141.

Foo, Josie. "Waiting" (story); "Garlanded Driftwood" (poem). *Open City* 1 (1992): 16–18.

Forché, Carolyn. "Refuge," "Prayer" (poems). *Open City* 17 (2003): 139–140.

Ford, Ford Madox. "Fun—It's Heaven!" (story). *Open City* 12 (2001): 305–310.

Foreman, Richard. "Eddie Goes to Poetry City" (excerpted story, drawings). *Open City* 2 (1993): 63–70.

Fox, Jason. "Models and Monsters" (paintings, drawings). *Open City* 17 (2003): 51–58.

Francis, Juliana. "The Baddest Natashas" (play). *Open City* 13 (2001): 149–172.

Friedman, Bruce Jay. "Lost" (story). *Open City* 16 (2002–2003): 185–190.

Friedman, Stan. "Male Pattern Baldness" (poem). *Open City* 1 (1992): 13–14.

Fuss, Adam. "Untitled" (photograph). *Open City* 6 (1998): front cover.

Gaddis, Anicée. "Fast and Slow" (story). *Open City* 20 (2005): 123–135.

Gaitskill, Mary. "The Crazy Person" (story). *Open City* 1 (1992): 49–61.

Gaitskill, Mary. "The Rubbed-Away Girl" (story). *Open City* 7 (1999): 137–148.

Gaffney, Elizabeth, trans., "Given" (story) by Alissa Walser. *Open City* 8 (1999): 141–149.

Galchen, Rivka. "Wild Berry Blue" (story). *Open City* 25 (2008): 69–84.

Ganay, Sebastien de. "Überfremdung" (paintings). *Open City* 11 (2000): 189–198.

Garrison, Deborah. "An Idle Thought," "Father, R.I.P., Sums Me Up at Twenty-Three," "A Friendship Enters Phase II" (poems). *Open City* 6 (1998): 21–26.

Garrison, Deborah. "Giving Notice" (letter). *Open City* 23 (2007): 79–80.

Garrison, Deborah. "A Short Skirt on Broadway," "Add One," "Both Square and Round," "The Necklace" (poems). *Open City* 23 (2007): 81–88.

Gerety, Meghan. Drawings. *Open City* 10 (2000): 151–158.

Gersh, Amanda. "On Safari" (story). *Open City* 10 (2000): 135–150.

Gifford, William. "Fight" (story). *Open City* 4 (1996): 207–214.

Gilbert, Josh. "Hack Wars" (story). *Open City* 18 (2003–2004): 55–60.

Gillick, Liam. "Signage for a Four Story Building" (art project). *Open City* 8 (1999): 121–125.

Gillison, Samantha. "Petty Cash" (story). *Open City* 4 (1996): 197–206.

Ginsberg, Allen. Photograph and text. *Open City* 3 (1995): 191–194.

Gizzi, Peter. "Take the 5:01 to Dreamland" (poem). *Open City* 17 (2003): 151–152.

Gold, Herbert. "Next In Line" (story). *Open City* 22 (2006): 65–69.

Goldstein, Jesse. "Dance With Me Ish, Like When You Was a Baby" (story). *Open City* 17 (2003): 197–199.

Golliver, Benjamin. "Las Vegas Bypass" (essay). *Open City* 26 (2008–2009): 121–130.

Gonzales, Mark. "To You, My Reader" (story). *Open City* 8 (1999): 153–154.

Harrison, Jim. "Arizona II" (story). *Open City* 23 (2007): 89–93.

Harrison, Jim. "Another Old Mariachi" (poem). *Open City* 23 (2007): 95.

Hart, JoeAnn. "Sawdust" (story). *Open City* 21 (2005–2006): 97–105.

Hartenbach, Mark. "emotional triage in assorted shapes & colors," "a two-toned oldsmobile going 85 mph," "sodium nitrate" (poems). *Open City* 24 (2007–2008): 69–71.

Harvey, Ellen. "Friends and Their Knickers" (paintings). *Open City* 6 (1998): 133–144.

Harvey, Ellen. "100 Visitors to the Biennial Immortalized" (drawings and text). *Open City* 25 (2008): 51–62.

Harvey, Matthea. "Sergio Valente, Sergio Valente, How You Look Tells the World How You Feel," "To Zanzibar By Motorcar" (poems). *Open City* 18 (2003–2004): 97–98.

Haug, James. "Everything's Jake" (poem). *Open City* 18 (2003–2004): 193.

Hauser, Thomas. "Schmetterlinge und Butterblumen" (drawings). *Open City* 12 (2001): 131–136.

Hayashi, Toru. "Equivocal Landscape" (drawings). *Open City* 12 (2001): 43–48.

Hayes, Michael. "Police Blotter." *Open City* 8 (1999): 107–110.

Healey, Steve. "The Asshole of the Immanent," "Tilt" (poems). *Open City* 15 (2002): 77–80.

Healy, Tom. "What the Right Hand Knows" (poem). *Open City* 17 (2003): 113–114.

Heeman, Christoph. "Pencil Drawings" (drawings). *Open City* 17 (2003): 91–98.

Hendriks, Martijn. "Swerve" (story). *Open City* 21 (2005–2006): 31–34.

Henry, Brian. "I Lost My Tooth on the Way to Plymouth (Rock)," "Intro to Lit" (poems). *Open City* 18 (2003–2004): 139–140.

Henry, Max and Sam Samore. "Hobo Deluxe, A Cinema of Poetry" (photographs and text). *Open City* 12 (2001): 257–270.

Henry, Peter. "Thrift" (poem). *Open City* 7 (1999): 136.

Hedegaard, Erik. "The La-Z-Boy Position" (story). *Open City* 4 (1996): 117–121.

Heyd, Suzanne. "Mouth Door I," "Mouth Door II" (poems). *Open City* 20 (2005): 175–179.

Higgs, Matthew. "Three Parts" and "Photograph of a Book (I Married an Artist)" (photographs). *Open City* 16 (2002–2003): 203–210; front and back covers.

Hill, Amy. "Psycho-narratives" (paintings). *Open City* 14 (2001–2002): 89–95.

Hillesland, Ann. "Ultimate Catch" (story). *Open City* 22 (2006): 37–47.

Hocking, Justin. "Dragon" (story). *Open City* 18 (2003–2004): 123–138.

Hoffman, Cynthia Marie. "Dear Commercial Street," (poem). *Open City* 17 (2003): 125–127.

Hofstede, Hilarius. "The Marquis Von Water" (text art project). *Open City* 3 (1995): 135–144.

Kay, Hellin. "Moscow & New York, Coming & Going" (photographs, story). *Open City* 15 (2002): 81–92.

Katchadourian, Nina. "Selections from *The Sorted Books Project*" (photographs). *Open City* 16 (2002–2003): 143–153.

Kazanas, Luisa. "Drawings" (drawings). *Open City* 13 (2001): 139–146.

Kean, Steve. Paintings. *Open City* 4 (1996): 129–133.

Keegan, Claire. "Surrender" (story). *Open City* 24 (2007–2008): 73–84.

Kenealy, Ryan. "Yellow and Maroon" (story). *Open City* 7 (1999): 60–70.

Kenealy, Ryan. "Resuscitation of the Shih Tzu" (story). *Open City* 16 (2002–2003): 89–96.

Kenealy, Ryan. "God's New Math" (story). *Open City* 20 (2005): 209–216.

Kennedy, Hunter. "Nice Cool Beds" (story). *Open City* 6 (1998): 162–174.

Kennedy, Hunter. "When Is It That You Feel Good?" (poem). *Open City* 9 (1999): 117–118.

Kennedy, Hunter. "Kitty Hawk" (story). *Open City* 12 (2001): 137–150.

Kharms, Daniil. "Case P-81210, Vol. 2, 1st Edition," "From Kharms's Journal," "A Humorous Division of the World in Half (Second Half)," "Blue Notebook No. 10" (poems). *Open City* 8 (1999): 130–136.

Kidd, Chip. Photographs. *Open City* 3 (1995): 129–133.

Kilimnick, Karen. "Untitled (Acid Is Groovy)" (photographs). *Open City* 9 (1999): 181–186; back cover.

Kim, Suji Kwock. "Aubade Ending with Lines from the Japanese" (poem). *Open City* 17 (2003): 117–118.

Kimball, Michael. "The Birds, the Light, Eating Breakfast, Getting Dressed, and How I Tried to Make It More of a Morning for My Wife" (story). *Open City* 20 (2005): 197–199.

Kinder, Chuck. "The Girl with No Face" (story). *Open City* 17 (2003): 31–38.

Kirby, Matthew. "The Lower Brudeckers" (story). *Open City* 22 (2006): 23–26.

Kirk, Joanna. "Clara" (drawings). *Open City* 11 (2000): 173–184.

Kleiman, Moe. "Tomorrow We Will Meet the Enemy" (poem). *Open City* 15 (2002): 119–120.

Klink, Joanna. "Lodestar" (poem). *Open City* 17 (2003): 109–110.

Knox, Jennifer L. "While Some Elegant Dancers Perched on Wires High Above a Dark, Dark Farm" (poem). *Open City* 19 (2004): 129–130.

Koestenbaum, Wayne. "First Dossier/Welcome Tour" (fiction/nonfiction). *Open City* 23 (2007): 115–124.

Koolhaas, Rem, with Harvard Project on the City. "Pearl River Delta, China" (photographs, graphs, text). *Open City* 6 (1998): 60–76.

Koons, Jeff. Photographs. *Open City* 1 (1992): 24–25.

Körmeling, John. "Drawings" (drawings). *Open City* 14 (2001–2002): 129–136.

Lemon, Alex. "Dourine," "Hallelujah Blackout" (poems). *Open City* 24 (2007–2008): 103–106.

Lesser, Guy. "The Good Sportsman, Et Cetera" (story). *Open City* 8 (1999): 75–86.

Levine, Margaret. "In a Dream It Happens," "Dilemma" (poems). *Open City* 16 (2002–2003): 159–160.

Lewinsky, Monica. "I Am a Pizza" (poem). *Open City* 6 (1998): 129.

Lewis, Jeremy. Introduction to "Happy Deathbeds." *Open City* 4 (1996): 49–52.

Lichtenstein, Miranda. "Stills from *The Naked City*" and "Untitled, #4 (Richardson Park)" (photographs). *Open City* 12 (2001): 275–284; front and back covers.

Lichtenstein, Miranda. "Ganzfeld" (photograph). *Open City* 21 (2005–2006): front and back covers.

Lida, David. "Bewitched" (story). *Open City* 9 (1999): 69–90.

Lindbloom, Eric. "Ideas of Order at Key West" (photographs). *Open City* 6 (1998): 155–161.

Lippman, Greg. "39 Gary Lippmans," "Lebenschluffen," "A Prize Subject for Diane Arbus," "Two Ears of Rice," "The Sound of Wine," "Fill 'Er Up" (poems). *Open City* 27 (2009): 123–128.

Lipsyte, Sam. "Shed" (story). *Open City* 3 (1995): 226–227.

Lipsyte, Sam. "Old Soul" (story). *Open City* 7 (1999): 79–84.

Lipsyte, Sam. "Cremains" (story). *Open City* 9 (1999): 167–176.

Lipsyte, Sam. "The Special Cases Lounge" (novel excerpt). *Open City* 13 (2001): 27–40.

Lipsyte, Sam. "Nate's Pain Is Now" (story). *Open City* 22 (2006): 1–8.

Longo, Giuseppe O. "In Zenoburg" (story), trans. David Mendel. *Open City* 12 (2001): 153–160.

Longo, Giuseppe O. "Rehearsal for a Deserted City" (story), trans. Martin Fawkes. *Open City* 15 (2002): 95–103.

Longo, Giuseppe O. "Conjectures about Hell" (story), trans. James B. Michels. *Open City* 25 (2008): 183–190.

Longo, Giuseppe O. "Braised Beef for Three" (story), trans. David Mendel. *Open City* 19 (2004): 135–148.

Lopate, Phillip. "Tea at the Plaza" (essay). *Open City* 21 (2005–2006): 15–20.

Lotbinière, Christopher de. Architectural drawings. *Open City* 27 (2009): 135–140.

Macklin, Elizabeth, trans., "The House Style," "A Qualifier of Superlatives" (poems). *Open City* 7 (1999): 107–111.

Macklin, Elizabeth, trans., "The River," "Visit" (poems) by Kirmen Uribe. *Open City* 17 (2003): 131–134.

Madoo, Ceres. "Drawings" (drawings). *Open City* 20 (2005): 149–154.

Malone, Billy. "Tanasitease" (drawings). *Open City* 21 (2005–2006): 91–96.

Malkmus, Steve. "Bennington College Rap" (poem). *Open City* 7 (1999): 46.

Mehmedinovic, Semezdin. "Hotel Room," "Precautionary Manifesto" (poems), trans. Ammiel Alcaly. *Open City* 17 (2003): 141–142.

Mehta, Diane. "Rezoning in Brooklyn" (poem). *Open City* 7 (1999): 71–72.

Mendel, David, trans., "In Zenoburg" (story) by Giuseppe O. Longo. *Open City* 12 (2001): 153–160.

Mendel, David, trans., "Braised Beef for Three" (story) by Giuseppe O. Longo. *Open City* 19 (2004): 135–148.

Mengestu, Dinaw. "Home at Last" (essay). *Open City* 24 (2007–2008): 107–112.

Merlis, Jim. "One Man's Theory" (story). *Open City* 10 (2000): 171–182.

Metres, Philip and Tatiana Tulchinsky, trans., "This Is Me" (poem) by Lev Rubinshtein. *Open City* 15 (2002): 121–134.

Michels, James B., trans., "Conjectures about Hell" (story) by Giuseppe O. Longo. *Open City* 25 (2008): 183–190.

Michels, Victoria Kohn. "At the Nightingale-Bamford School for Girls" (poem). *Open City* 4 (1996): 166–167.

Middlebrook, Jason. "APL #1 Polar Bear" (drawing). *Open City* 18 (2003–2004): front and back covers.

Milford, Kate. Photographs. *Open City* 2 (1993): 54–56.

Milford, Matthew. "Civil Servants" (paintings, text). *Open City* 7 (1999): 47–55.

Miller, Greg. "Intercessor" (poem). *Open City* 11 (2000): 51.

Miller, Jane. "From *A Palace of Pearls*" (poem). *Open City* 17 (2003): 157–160.

Miller, Matt. "Driver" (poem). *Open City* 12 (2001): 169–170.

Miller, Matt. "Chimera" (poem). *Open City* 21 (2005–2006): 119–120.

Miller, Stephen Paul. "When Listening to the Eighteen-and-a-Half Minute Tape Gap as Electronic Music" (poem). *Open City* 4 (1996): 162.

M.I.M.E. Photographs. *Open City* 9 (1999): 207–218.

Mobilio, Albert. "Adhesiveness: There Was This Guy" (story). *Open City* 5 (1997): 55–56.

Moeckel, Thorpe. "Johnny Stinkbait Bears His Soul" (story). *Open City* 23 (2007): 157–162.

Moeckel, Thorpe. "Dream of My Father," "Nature Poem, Inc.," "Mussels," "At the Co-op," "Beautiful Jazz" (poems). *Open City* 23 (2007): 163–171.

Moody, Rick. "Dead Man Writes," "Domesticity," "Immortality," "Two Sonnets for Stacey" (poems). *Open City* 6 (1998): 83–88.

Moore, Honor. "She Remembers," "The Heron" (poems). *Open City* 13 (2001): 71–78.

Moore, Honor. "In Place of an Introduction" (assemblage). *Open City* 17 (2003): 105–106.

Moore, Honor. "Homage," "Hotel Brindisi," "Tango" (poems). *Open City* 20 (2005): 77–80.

Rubinshtein, Lev. "This Is Me" (poem), trans. Philip Metres and Tatiana Tulchinsky. *Open City* 15 (2002): 121–134.

Rubinstein, Raphael, trans., "From *Letter to Antonio Saura*" (story) by Marcel Cohen. *Open City* 17 (2003): 217–225.

Ruda, Ed. "The Seer" (story). *Open City* 1 (1992): 15.

Ruppersberg, Allen. "Greetings from L.A." (novel). *Open City* 16 (2002–2003): throughout.

Rush, George. "Interior, Exterior, Portrait, Still-Life, Landscape" (print). *Open City* 19 (2004): 73–83.

Ruvo, Christopher. "Afternoon, 1885" (poem). *Open City* 18 (2003–2004): 185–186.

Rux, Carl Hancock. "Geneva Cottrell, Waiting for the Dog to Die" (play). *Open City* 13 (2001): 189–213.

Šalamun, Tomaž. "VI," "VII" (poems), trans. author and Joshua Beckman. *Open City* 15 (2002): 155–157.

Šalamun, Tomaž. "Porcini," "Spring Street" (poems), trans. author and Joshua Beckman. *Open City* 27 (2009):147–150 .

Salmon, Audrey. "Mutant Architecture" (art project). *Open City* 27 (2009): 51–60.

Salvatore, Joseph. "Practice Problem" (story). *Open City* 7 (1999): 127–135.

Samore, Sam and Max Henry. "Hobo Deluxe, A Cinema of Poetry" (photographs and text). *Open City* 12 (2001): 257–270.

Samton, Matthew. "Y2K, or How I Learned to Stop Worrying and Love the CD-Rom" (poem). *Open City* 12 (2001): 191–196.

Saroyan, Strawberry. "Popcorn" (story). *Open City* 6 (1998): 125–128.

Saroyan, Strawberry. "Strawberry Is" (poem). *Open City* 26 (2008–2009): 73–80.

Sayrafiezadeh, Saïd. "My Mother and the Stranger" (story). *Open City* 17 (2003): 59–66.

Schaeffer, Doug. "Withdrawn" (collages). *Open City* 24 (2007–2008): 93–98 and back cover.

Schleinstein, Bruno. "Drawings" (drawings). *Open City* 17 (2003): 227–237.

Schles, Ken. Two untitled photographs. *Open City* 1 (1992): front and back covers.

Schles, Ken. Photography. *Open City* 2 (1993): front cover.

Schles, Ken. Two photographs. *Open City* 10 (2000): front and back covers.

Schles, Ken. "New York City: Street Photographs Following the Terrorist Attack on the World Trade Center, September 2001" (photographs). *Open City* 14 (2001–2002): 219–232.

Schmidt, Elizabeth. "Crossing Chilmark Pond," "Quiet Comfort" (poems). *Open City* 26 (2008–2009): 25–31.

Schneider, Ryan. "Mattress," "I Will Help You Destroy This, World" (poems). *Open City* 18 (2003–2004): 249–250.

Skinner, Jeffrey. "Winn-Dixie," "Survey Says," "Video Vault" (poems). *Open City* 8 (1999): 69–74.

Sledge, Michael. "The Birdlady of Houston" (story). *Open City* 16 (2002–2003): 211–221.

Smith, Charlie. "A Selection Process," "Agents of the Moving Company," "Evasive Action" (poems). *Open City* 6 (1998): 43–46.

Smith, Lee. Two untitled poems. *Open City* 3 (1995): 224–225.

Smith, Lee. "The Balsawood Man" (story). *Open City* 10 (2000): 203–206.

Smith, Molly. "untitled (underlie)" (drawings). *Open City* 21 (2005–2006): 41–48.

Smith, Peter Nolan. "Why I Miss Junkies" (story). *Open City* 13 (2001): 115–129.

Smith, Peter Nolan. "Better Lucky Than Good" (story). *Open City* 19 (2004): 65–70.

Smith, Rod. "Sandaled" (poem). *Open City* 14 (2001–2002): 145.

Snyder, Rick. "No Excuse," "Pop Poem '98" (poems). *Open City* 8 (1999): 151–152.

Smith, Dean. "Head Fake" (poem). *Open City* 1 (1992): 19–20.

Smith, Scott. "The Egg Man" (story). *Open City* 20 (2005): 1–67.

Solotaroff, Ivan. "Love Poem (On 53rd and 5th)" (poem). *Open City* 3 (1995): 228.

Solotaroff, Ivan. "Prince of Darkness" (story). *Open City* 6 (1998): 97–114.

Solotroff, Mark. "Fe·nes·tral Drawings" (drawings). *Open City* 18 (2003–2004): 213–218.

Southern, Nile. "Cargo of Blasted Mainframes" (story, drawings). *Open City* 1 (1992): 62–70.

Southern, Terry. "Twice on Top" (screenplay). *Open City* 2 (1993): 82–92.

Southern, Terry. "*C'est Toi Alors*: Scenario for Existing Props and French Cat" (screenplay). *Open City* 13 (2001): 41–43.

Space3. "Street Report EHV 003-2001" (prints). *Open City* 15 (2002): 159–164.

Spain, Chris. "The Least Wrong Thing" (story). *Open City* 26 (2008–2009): 33–52.

Specktor, Matthew. "A King in Mirrors" (story). *Open City* 26 (2008–2009): 59–72.

Staffel, Tim. "December 24, 1999–January 1, 2000" (story), trans. Elke Siegel and Paul Fleming. *Open City* 12 (2001): 95–118.

Stahl, Jerry. "Gordito" (story). *Open City* 22 (2006): 9–14.

Starkey, David. "Poem to Beer" (poem). *Open City* 12 (2001): 73–72.

Stefans, Brian Kim. "Two Pages from *The Screens*" (poem). *Open City* 14 (2001–2002): 163–165.

Stefans, Cindy. Photographs. *Open City* 6 (1998): 37–42.

OPEN CITY

Torn, Jonathan. "Arson" (story). *Open City* 1 (1992): 10–12.

Torn, Tony. "Hand of Dust," "Farmers: 3 a.m.," "To Mazatlan" (poems). *Open City* 10 (2000): 225–230.

Tosches, Nick. "My Kind of Loving" (poem). *Open City* 4 (1996): 23.

Tosches, Nick. "*L'uccisore e la Farfalla*," "*Ex Tenebris, Apricus*," "I'm in Love with Your Knees," "A Cigarette with God" (poems). *Open City* 13 (2001): 45–55.

Tosches, Nick. "Proust and the Rat" (story). *Open City* 16 (2002–2003): 223–226.

Tosches, Nick. "Gynæcology" (poem). *Open City* 18 (2003–2004): 165–166.

Tosches, Nick. "The Lectern at Helicarnassus" (poem). *Open City* 21 (2005–2006): 165.

Toulouse, Sophie. "Sexy Clowns" (photographs). *Open City* 17 (2003): 201–208.

Tower, Jon. Photographs, drawings, and text. *Open City* 1 (1992): 79–86.

Trubek, Anne and Laura Larson. "Genius Loci" (photographs, text). *Open City* 7 (1999): 85–94.

Tulchinsky, Tatiana and Paul Metres, trans., "This Is Me" (poem) by Lev Rubinshtein. *Open City* 15 (2002): 121–134.

Turner, Ben Carlton. "Composition Field 1," "Composition Field 2," "Soft-Core Porno" (poems). *Open City* 25: 123–130.

Uklanski, Piotr. "Queens" (photograph). *Open City* 8 (1999): front and back covers.

Uribe, Kirmen. "The River," "Visit" (poems) trans. Elizabeth Macklin. *Open City* 17 (2003): 131–134.

Vapnyar, Lara. "Mistress" (story). *Open City* 15 (2002): 135–153.

Vapnyar, Lara. "There Are Jews in My House" (story). *Open City* 17 (2003): 243–273.

Vicente, Esteban. Paintings. *Open City* 3 (1995): 75–80.

Vicuña, Cecilia. "The Brilliance of Orifices," "Mother of Pearl," "The Anatomy of Paper" (poems), trans. Rosa Alcalá. *Open City* 14 (2001–2002): 151–154.

Walker, Wendy. "Sophie in the Catacombs" (story). *Open City* 19 (2004): 131–132.

Wallace, David Foster. "Nothing Happened" (story). *Open City* 5 (1997): 63–68.

Walls, Jack. "Hi-fi" (story). *Open City* 13 (2001): 237–252.

Walser, Alissa. "Given" (story), trans. Elizabeth Gaffney. *Open City* 8 (1999): 141–150.

Walsh, J. Patrick III. "It's time to go out on your own." (drawings). *Open City* 19 (2004): 35–40.

Wareck, Sarah Borden. "The Ambassador's Daughter" (story). *Open City* 25 (2008): 107–122.

Willis, Elizabeth. "Devil Bush," "Of Which I Shall Have Occasion to Speak Again" (poems). *Open City* 21 (2005–2006): 29–30.

Wilson, Tim. "Private Beach Bitches" (story). *Open City* 16 (2002–2003): 193–199.

Winer, Jody. "Mrs. Sherlock Holmes States Her Case," "How to Arrive at a Motel" (poems). *Open City* 11 (2000): 141–144.

Wolff, Rebecca. "Chinatown, Oh" (poem). *Open City* 5 (1997): 35–37.

Wolff, Rebecca. "Mom Gets Laid" (poem). *Open City* 9 (1999): 177–180.

Wolff, Rebecca. "The Beginners" (story). *Open City* 23 (2007): 225–237.

Wolff, Rebecca. "Literary Agency," "My Daughter," "Only Rhubarb," "The Reductions," "Who Can I Ask for an Honest Assessment?" (poems). *Open City* 23 (2007): 239–243.

Woodman, Francesca. Untitled photographs. *Open City* 3 (1995): 229–234 and back cover.

Wormwood, Rick. "Burt and I" (story). *Open City* 9 (1999): 129–140.

Wormser, Baron. "Annals of Allegory #36," "Fantasia on Three Sentences from a Letter by Robert Lowell" (poems). *Open City* 24 (2007–2008): 113–117.

Woychuk-Mlinac, Ava. "Why?" (poem). *Open City* 19 (2004): 179.

Yankelevich, Matvei, trans., "Who By Fire" (story) by Victor Pelevin. *Open City* 7 (1999): 95–106.

Yankelevich, M. E. Introduction to Daniil Kharms. *Open City* 8 (1999): 127–129.

Yankelevich, Matvei. "The Green Bench" (poem). *Open City* 19 (2004): 149–150.

Yas, Joanna. "Boardwalk" (story). *Open City* 10 (2000): 95–102.

Yates, Richard. "Uncertain Times" (unfinished novel). *Open City* 3 (1995): 35–71.

Yau, John. "Forbidden Entries" (story). *Open City* 2 (1993): 75–76.

Young, Kevin. "Encore," "Sorrow Song," "Saxophone Solo," "Muzak" (poems). *Open City* 16 (2002–2003): 121–127.

Zaitzeff, Amine. "Westchester Burning" (story). *Open City* 8 (1999): 45–68.

Zapruder, Matthew. "The Pajamaist" (poem). *Open City* 21 (2005–2006): 35–39.

Zumas, Leni. "Dragons May Be the Way Forward" (story). *Open City* 22 (2006): 15–22.

Zwahlen, Christian. "I Want You to Follow Me Home" (story). *Open City* 19 (2004): 27–32.